3765300287374
Main Library:
FIC PECK
Martin and John : a novel

APR 9 3

**CENTRAL ARKANSAS LIBRARY SYSTEM
LITTLE ROCK PUBLIC LIBRARY
700 LOUISIANA ST.
LITTLE ROCK, AR**

GAYLORD

MARTIN AND JOHN

THIS BOOK IS FOR

JOY LINSCHEID

AND

BRUCE MORROW

CENTRAL ARKANSAS LIBRARY SYSTEM
LITTLE ROCK PUBLIC LIBRARY
700 LOUISIANA STREET
LITTLE ROCK, ARKANSAS 72201

ACKNOWLEDGMENTS

FOR THEIR SUPPORT, inspiration, and comments, I thank: Elizabeth Allen, Fenella Barton, Damien Boisvert, Jean-Claude Breach, Janet Burstein, Pito Callas, John Campanelli, C. B. Cooke, Dennis Cooper, Diane Ferrara, John Figueroa, Suzanne Gardinier, my editor John Glusman, Sarah Goldstein, Tasha Harris, Dennis Hunter, Amanda Johnson, Chris Johnson, Joyce Johnson, Eric Latzky, Micki Lennon, Derek Link, Joy, Barry Lowenthal, Bruce, Bob Ready, my agent Irene Skolnick, Roger Schulte, Helen Schulman, Deb Schwartz, Alexandra Shapiro, George Stambolian, Greg Vernice, Jim Wagner, Scott Wilson (both of them), and Wahn Yoon.

Copyright © 1993 by Dale Peck
All rights reserved
Printed in the United States of America
Published simultaneously in Canada by HarperCollinsCanadaLtd
Designed by Fritz Metsch
First edition, 1993

LIBRARY OF CONGRESS CATALOGING-IN-PUBLICATION DATA
Peck, Dale.
Martin and John: a novel / Dale Peck.—1st ed.
p. cm.
I. Title.
PS3566.E245M37 1993
813'.54—dc20   92-1622 CIP

MARTIN AND JOHN

A

NOVEL

DALE

PECK

FARRAR · STRAUS · GIROUX
NEW YORK

93 04055

The water is wide,
I cannot swim o'er,
and neither have I
wings with which to fly.

Oh, give me a boat
that can carry two,
and both shall row,
my love and I.

MARTIN AND JOHN

HERE IS THIS

BABY

I

"Here is this baby, crying in my arms, and don't he know just when to stop? He's been crying all day, and not just in my arms. I'm a busy woman, can't be carrying a baby around all day, and this house don't clean itself, I'll tell you that much. And it don't matter if I hold him, or lay him in his crib in our room, which is quiet during the day, or put him in front of the TV—it don't matter, he still cries. And I'll tell you this too: there isn't a woman I know can listen to her own baby cry for eight hours straight and not pick it up once in a while, and not get mad sometimes, and have to bite her lip to keep from yelling, and not think maybe something besides this ninety-degree heat and hundred-degree humidity is wrong. So I made the mistake of calling his father. And don't you just know Henry? First of all he said, 'Bea, I told you not to bother me at work.' And then he told me, 'Ain't nothing wrong with John. Ain't nothing wrong with my son.' I tell you, sometimes it's not too much to believe that when they cut the cord off me they attached it to him. But what's the use in thinking like that?

"Well, listen, I put a wet cloth on John's head, and he pulled the end of it into his mouth and sucked on it for a little bit, and that seemed to help. But I have to tell you that he didn't really stop crying until just now, until the car door slammed in the driveway, until the storm door slammed in the other room. And I'm not saying that John heard this, and I'm not saying he understood it either, but I'll be damned if he's not shutting up at just the right time, lying in my arms with his eyes wide open and innocent like he hasn't done a thing, and don't he just know who's going to get it now?"

BLUE WET - PAINT

COLUMNS

I

This is not the worst thing I remember: coming home from school one day to find my mother in a chair, collapsed. Her skin was the color of wet ashes, her head sat like a stone on her right shoulder, and a damp bloody mass pushed at her crotch, staining a maroon patch of darkness on sky-blue pants. Her legs were spread wide, and more blood, pooling on the yellow vinyl of the chair, showed up like the red speck in a spoiled egg yolk. Her arms were open too, and rested on the chair arms, and she seemed both empty and full, like a tube of toothpaste squeezed from the middle. When I walked into the room, I was ten years old, and the sound her blood made as it dropped to the floor filled my ears. Is she still alive? I remember thinking, and then, when I noticed the slow, small movements of her chest, I thought, She still isn't dead. I ran into the living room then, where I called my father, and I waited for him on the couch, shivering. Not seeing her was worse than seeing her, for I imagined her, imagined the mound that had been building in her abdomen for months.

It had grown even as the rest of her body had shrunk, until she seemed nothing more than a skeleton covered by the thin fabric of clothing and skin. Just a skeleton, and that hard mound at her center, which my father sometimes ran his hands over as though testing a melon for ripeness. For years I saw that melon drop from my mother's body again and again, pushing at the seam of her pants in a mess of blood and guts and lost life. Not the baby's—my mother's.

This story started before I was aware of it. Though two people were in a position to tell it, they were both, I believe, unable to speak. How could my mother, a housewife who remembered her high school graduation as a severe bout of morning sickness, sit me on her lap and say, "John, your father is killing me," when speaking would reveal at least some level of complicity on her part? And how could my father, a construction worker who lucked into a lot of money when he opened his own company, sit me down and say, "John, all we can do is wait for her to die," when he knew it was his fault she was dying? So no one said anything—I wasn't even told my mother had miscarried, and no attempt was made to explain why I'd found her sitting in her own blood. In time my father referred to it as if I knew what had happened. "When your mother lost the baby," he'd say, as if she'd set it down, forgotten where. Other things were set down with that baby, forgotten, and one of them was the woman who

6

bore it: my mother, whose black-and-white past was obliter-
ated by that technicolor moment in the kitchen. A too-bright
image superimposed itself on a dark one and only occasionally
could a piece of that hidden picture reveal itself.

Over time I learned that my mother's miscarriage was the
product of a muscle disorder that lay dormant for years, waiting for something like the strain of bearing a baby to flare
up. Someone once told me she'd been ill after my birth, but
when I asked my father about it he only said, "You got out
of the hospital before she did." Now, looking back, this and
a half dozen other signals pop up like road signs pointing to
her illness. She was always dropping things: glasses held in
both her hands still managed to slip to the floor, and forkfuls
of food spilled to her lap on the way to her mouth. If she
was tired this got worse, and sometimes, late at night, her
speech became slurred, though she never drank with my
father. When she got pregnant, her deterioration accelerated.
My father joked it off: "Rosemary," he'd say—her name was
Beatrice—"and her baby," and on the last word he'd rub the
mound of her stomach. My mother never laughed at this, I
noticed at once, but it took me a while to see that my father
didn't either. She'd turn back to what she was doing, cooking
dinner maybe, or copying a recipe from a magazine. Years
later, a flip through her card file revealed the definite progression of her disease: her handwriting started out smooth
and rolling, and then in the years just before she miscarried

it began to jumble about frantically like the lines of an EKG. And then gradually, inevitably, it became as flat as stagnant water.

In a way, all I know now is all I knew then: that she suffered from a progressive muscle disorder which destroyed her motor control and left her a quadriplegic, unable to walk or speak or hold her head up; this disease actually killed her when she was forty-four years old, but for the last twelve years of her life she was in a facility on the eastern edge of Long Island, a hospice, while my father and I lived fifteen hundred miles away in Kansas, and it often seems like she died when she was only thirty-two. She was twenty-nine when she came home from the hospital for the first time, in a wheelchair. This eventually gave way to a whining electric one, but at the time she was too weak to work a joystick and had to be pushed around by my father. When I heard the car in the driveway that day, my first impulse was to hide, but I forced myself into the living room just as the front door slammed open. All I saw was my father's shadowy form, huge, hulking, framed by late-afternoon light, leaning over my mother. At first I thought she'd fallen, but then I realized she was sitting, and then I realized she sat in a wheelchair. Her body was displayed as it had been in the kitchen chair—legs wide, spine bent, head on one shoulder—but it seemed this time she was huddling in fear, not collapsed from weakness. Then my father stood up—he'd had to lean over her to push open the door—and the light brought out concern in his face, and fear, which he tried to smile away. "Look, Mom," he said, "it's John." My mother's head raised slowly, as if an invisible fisherman had hooked her forehead and was reeling in carefully so as not to tear the skin. She smiled and breathed a greeting so quietly that I didn't hear it. I wish now that I'd pressed my ear against her, listening as though for a heartbeat. There were so few words afterward that I curse myself now for each one I missed while I hid in my room. But I was frightened, both by her new emaciated state, and by my father. It's not that he threatened me, or forced me away— not physically anyway—but I could never overcome the eager, easy way he expressed his concern for her. It made me feel cold, inhuman.

He visited her every day in the hospital; I never went. When she came home he began to work out of our house, and he cared for her alone. He'd bring her in the living room when he watched TV and hold her body while she slept or stared blankly at the wall. And I'll never forget the way he ran to the kitchen the day I found her, tripping over things like a blind man. He stood in the door for a long time. I don't think he noticed me—he stared only at her. Then, as if he'd fallen, he was on his knees before her, arms thrown around her waist, pants and shirtfront soiled with her blood. His sobs shook the air in the room, though they didn't rouse her, and he kept repeating, "Oh, Bea, I'm sorry, I'm so sorry." He repeated it so many times that even at ten years old I realized his apology might hold a deeper meaning, a message he directed to me as much as to my mother: he told her he was sorry, but he looked at me when he spoke, and if grief was what poured, no *shone*, from him with the intensity of light, then guilt—visible, visceral, unavoidable guilt—was the sun from which this other emotion radiated. Grief was the white line that ringed each pupil of my father's wide eyes, but guilt was the dark hole that burned at their centers, and the sight of it scared me so much that I closed my eyes and curled my body into a ball, refusing to open them until long after the first of two ambulances that came for my mother during her lifetime had taken her away. When it had gone, my father put my curled-up form to bed. His breathing filled the room for a few moments after he'd set me down and then, after I heard the door close behind him, the room— and the house—seemed as quiet as the bottom of the ocean.

And this is where everything starts, at least for me. But for my parents, I now realize, things began long before. I know because of our leather recliner. In my memory my mother is always sitting—in the kitchen chair, in her wheelchair, in my father's recliner, where he held her when he watched TV. On the day I'm remembering, my mother sits in it alone, stiff, her hand in the air holding a lit cigarette. Her cheeks seem gaunt, her hair flat and stringy, and when she says she needs to tell me something and asks me to sit on her lap I don't want to, I want to avoid her, the way children avoid sick people. But I go to her anyway. "You remember how we talked about having a baby brother or sister one day?" my mother says as I settle myself. And then, without waiting for an answer, she says, "I went to the doctor today. He told me I can't have another baby." She sucks on her cigarette, puts it out. The ashtray is full, and she has to push the butts out of the way before she can grind this one out. "It wouldn't be good for me, he said. I could get sick, real sick." I listen to her but don't know what to think. Her breath smells bad, her legs feel hard—bony—beneath me. I wait for her to say something that will tell me how to feel but she just sets me down suddenly, takes the ashtray to the kitchen, empties and washes it, and then she makes me a sandwich. "Don't worry about it," she tells me while I eat. "Your father and I will worry about it." That night, all night, they argue. "But we want a big family," my father says again and again. "That doesn't matter now," my mother answers each time, but each time her voice is quieter, weaker, until finally it doesn't come at all. Then there is just my father's voice. "We want a big family," he says one last time, and then he says, "Come on, let's go to bed." And in the present tense that is childhood —or, at any rate, that was my childhood—I didn't connect those words with the ones my mother had spoken that afternoon, just as, months later, I wouldn't connect them to my mother in the kitchen chair. I simply heard my parents arguing, and all I wanted was for them to stop. I didn't care how they stopped, and I didn't care why, and I certainly didn't care what happened after they went to bed.

*　　*　　*

On the night my mother died, a hard dry wind was blowing in off the ocean. You'd think that a west-moving wind would carry moisture, but it didn't: it was dry and gritty as sandpaper, the kind of wind that blows in Kansas. It bit my cheeks as I hailed a cab, and inside the car, hot dusty air filled my throat. The air gave the city a grainy impression, and I found myself looking for a hidden camera recording me, the only child on the way to retrieve his mother's last effects. If someone asked about her, I used to say that she was dead, she died a long time ago, I don't even remember what she looked like. But my mother's face hides just behind mine; I need only glimpse myself and I see her, and every memory I have of her life before she went to the hospice. I know nothing of her life since then. This was my doing, not hers: just before she left I asked her not to mail any letters she might write. She couldn't write actually, but the hospice had told us that some-one would write for her. It was a month before her thirty-second birthday, I remember. My present to her was a ring she'd given me eight years earlier, when I was five. The ring was plain and silver and not very wide to start with, and over the years it had become thin as a wire as repeated trips to the jeweler to resize it sacrificed the band's width for diameter. I remember sliding the band off my index finger and then, holding my mother's hand carefully, I uncurled her middle finger and slipped it on her. When I was done, I set her hand back in her lap, and the finger with the ring remained ex-tended even as her other fingers curled with illusory force into her palm. My mother's mouth twitched into a smile and her head fell over in her excitement. I pushed it up for her. By then communication was only an approximation for her; she couldn't control her vocal cords, and it had become almost impossible for her to type, a letter at a time, with a long thin bar fastened to a band on her wrist. But if communication was hard for her, it seemed harder for my father and me: she knew what she wanted to say; we were the ones who had to struggle to figure out what she meant. This was why she was going away—to "finish dying" in a place where my father and I wouldn't constantly be saying, What is it, Bea? what do you want, Mom? what do you mean? I gave her the ring early because, by the time her birthday came, she would be gone: enshrined, entombed, encoded in a place that for the next dozen years I'd think of only as a dot on the far edge of a Long Island road map. I remember I waited until she was able to focus her eyes on me. "I want you to write," I said then, and then I added, "but please don't mail the letters." One sentence, two independent clauses, and I stopped. If pressed, I'd have said I didn't want to reassemble her like a jigsaw puzzle, each letter a tiny piece that arrived one at a time. What frightened me was the idea that my mother's life could endlessly fade, but never end. When I told her not to mail her letters, I was really telling her something else, and I wonder if she knew what that was: that I didn't want to think about her again—until after she died.

When the ambulance came to take her to the hospice, my

father took me to the prairie. Everything had already been sold or shipped or packed in the car, and so, just minutes after the ambulance pulled away, lights on but siren off, we left. My last image of my mother, really, is the back of that ambulance. The impression stayed with me throughout our drive, and I couldn't shake the idea that my mother would be in the ambulance forever, moving from place to place. Sometimes I believed that my father and I also lacked a destination: we drove for days and days—really only two or three, but in the enclosed monotony of the car I lost track of time. I slept and woke, slept and woke, and each time I opened my eyes I asked my father, "Are we in another state yet?" Usually he said, "No, we're still in the same state," though sometimes he said, "We're in Ohio now," or Illinois, or Indiana. During the trip, he only allowed his hands to leave the steering wheel to adjust the radio. With his eyes fixed on the road ahead of him, his fingers would fumble with the tuner knob like a blind man's, and sometimes, when he punched the program buttons, he got only static: those old stations were long gone. When he finally found music without words he left the needle there, and on its way back to the steering wheel his hand would make a detour to squeeze my knee. When he touched me like that I clambered into the back seat. We drove one of those big American things from the seventies, but already I was too tall to stretch out fully and had to put my feet up on the window. These are my clearest memories of our trip: lying on my back and looking through the angled glass of the rear window at the lighted signs of buildings as they flashed overhead, and at long slabs of pine-covered mountains which darkened the glass, and, later, at grassy hills which seemed to unroll endlessly, as though off a spindle. The images reflected in the window were transparent, and with an effort I could look through them and see empty sky, and in that emptiness I believed I saw the real reason for all this scenery, these miles, these hours in the car: emptying the mind. The hills, mountains, and buildings vanished behind us as we passed them, and I forgot them, and I tried to forget the past as well. But my father resisted. Once, at a diner, he said, "She's probably having breakfast right now." I broke the yolk of my egg and watched the yellow ooze take over the plate. "What do you think she's eating?" he asked. I didn't answer, and my father went on without waiting. "Grapefruit maybe," he said, "and eggs and sausages, or toast with butter and jelly. Maybe grits if they get into Southern cooking. Did you see they had grits on the menu here?" I nodded my head, eyes down, looking at the food I kept my mouth full of so I wouldn't have to speak. My mother couldn't chew: she was probably being spoon-fed oatmeal. While he spoke, my father played with his meal. He moved the two eggs to the top of his plate, put the potato patty in the center, the bacon in a crooked curve at the bottom. He combed the sprig of parsley with his fingers and put it above the eggs, and then he rotated the plate one hundred and eighty degrees. "Looks like her a little, don't you think?" I had no food left to put in my mouth, no excuse for not answering, but I couldn't, there was nothing to say. I looked at him. His expression was impossible to read, and I have to wonder now if he was thinking about her or about what he'd done to her. "The nose is a little too big," he said finally, and tried to laugh. I looked at his plate. The "face" breathed steam, and gray wisps dispersed in the air like the conversation my father and I weren't having. We sat in the restaurant, a diner—fifty miles farther west and it would be called a café—and we looked at each other over the dead yellow eyes until a waitress came by and my father had her take the plate away, and then we drove the rest of the way to our new home, in Kansas.

I hadn't known where we were going when we left, and I didn't know we'd arrived when we got there. Only a concrete slab in the middle of a vast treeless field marked the site of our house, and we ate our first meals there on a picnic table in the center of it. Though my father bought some food in restaurants, he usually barbecued, and when he did he wore an old, old apron whose yellow ruffles, darkened by dust trapped in their creases, trailed around his knees. The men building our house teased me about this. "Your old man wears the pants in the family, huh?" they'd say while my father was busy flipping burgers. I'd just look at them until they finished. "And the dress!" they'd guffaw, and slap each other on the back. When they saw I wasn't laughing, they'd relent and say, "Aw, but you're okay, John, anybody can see that." They only talked to my father to complain about the lack of a floor plan. "Just put a wall there," my father would say with a construction foreman's bellow. "I know what I'm doing," he'd say. "I was working construction when you were still sucking your mother's tit." He said these words as if they lacked a literal meaning, as if their only purpose was to show the workers who was boss. His yells earned him a grudging respect, but the beers he'd hand out at the end of the day served him better. "Just a couple to start you on your way," he'd say. At first I thought he meant on their way home, but soon I realized that he meant on their way to being drunk, and later I came to see another meaning lurking behind his words: the men who worked for my father were young, all newly married or about to be married, and those beers he handed out, and the bawdy stories he told them as I hid and listened—stories that were sometimes about my mother— were sending them all on their way to the place in which he'd lived for years, a place in which men sometimes got blind drunk, and did things, and in the morning felt only their own pain, and not the pain they'd caused. Late on those nights, as my father slept next to me in a tent on the cement floor, I'd listen to the sounds he made, which were amplified by the incredible silence of the prairie surrounding us. He snored, cried, ground his teeth, and, in his sleep, said, "I'm sorry." He was still sorry. It was during those nights that I let myself wonder for the first time since my mother's miscarriage if my father was actually asking forgiveness for something he'd done. But I never pushed that thought very far. Usually I was distracted by the erection that pulsed between my legs—I was thirteen then, and more than I wanted to know why my father kept repeating "I'm sorry," I wanted a place to masturbate. Every night I pressed the fingernails of my left hand into the fingertips of my right. I'd press hard, until my right hand ached, and I concentrated on that pain until it was all I could feel, or hear, or remember.

"People do bad things," he said once. I don't remember why we were talking, or under what circumstances, but I remember that he was drunk. "It's so common it's almost not important. What's important is what they do afterward." "You mean how they try to make up for it?" I said. "I mean *if* they try to make up for it. I mean, you can't ever make up for hurting a person like that, but if you don't try, then you're twice as low." Something went cold in me then. The pieces of the puzzle fell together before I could stop them, and the picture they made was of my mother in the kitchen chair. I looked at my father differently after that. His grieving, his guilt, the things he did to remember her—it all started to seem like a bad TV movie. Like the way he cooked up a storm after the house was finished. He still worked in her apron, which he'd washed, and he was usually hard at it by the time I got home from school. "How was your day?" he'd call from the kitchen as I came in. "Fine," I'd say, "but I'm on my way—" "Come here," my father interrupted me. "Can you read your mother's handwriting?" In the kitchen, my father held a recipe card. I looked at it. "Meatloaf," I read, and tried to hand the card back to him. "I know that," he said. "It's the recipe I can't read." I looked at the card again, at the whorls and scribbles and seemingly random slashes and dots that were supposed to be letters, words. "Ground beef," I read aloud. "Medium . . . medium cracker crumbs. Tomato soup—no, not soup, sauce." He listened to the words as if they were a homily I was translating from Latin. "One more time," he said when I finished. "I want to make sure I've got it." I paused. "Look, why don't you write this down?" "Why?" he said. "I've got the card. And I've got you." He'd turned away and I looked at his back now, at the knot of the apron which sat just above the worn leather of his work belt. "A pound and a half of ground beef," I said. "But it says to use less if you're cooking for two."

Sometimes he fed the finished dishes to me and the girl I dated then, Susan. Sometimes when we were sitting in the living room, waiting for something to come out of the oven, he broke off in the middle of a sentence and just stared at us, and his wet eyes held answers to questions I didn't want to ask, or be asked by Susan. Soon I started to avoid our house. Our town was tiny and there was nothing to see in it; inevitably, the prairie drew me. Nothing on Long Island had prepared me for the long wind-smoothed rolls of land which surrounded our new house. Tall brown grass covered everything. The grass had a dull side and a shiny side, and when the wind blew, the grass rippled and the sun flashed as though off glass, or water. Seeing that, I reached back and imagined the prairie as the sea it once was, and I imagined myself on the first island to raise itself above the water's surface. I stood there in mud fast drying under the sun. As I watched, all the water retreated under the land around me, and then for a time there was nothing except me and the naked wet soil, and we waited for the wind to carry the first seeds there, we waited for the grass to grow and cover us like a blanket.

There was a place out there called the red cliffs. When I first saw them, they reminded me of my dream. The cliffs were like a gash in the earth, eons old but still raw, and their exposed soil was red as if it had just been soaked in blood. Susan took me there. We walked through a fallow pasture; the prairie grasses came to our waist so we high-stepped, and I remember shivering in the cold wind that blew at our backs. At a barbed wire fence Susan stepped on the third strand and pulled up the second, and I crawled through and held the fence for her. On the other side the grass bunched in chewed clumps, and in many places the ground was bare, as if the grass had been pulled out by the roots. "Sheep," Susan said derisively. "They graze a field to death." The only thing that had escaped were a few prickly pear cacti crouched with their long needles rigidly displayed. Susan picked an ugly brown pod off one of them and forced it open. Five pale blue petals blew from her hand. "Their flowers," she said. "They only bloom when it rains." It wasn't love that filled me then, but wonder that she should know these things: awe. I took her hand awkwardly, and we walked the rest of the way in silence on an old cow path that must have been there before they brought in the sheep. Something about the prairie forces your eye down: it's like your mind is trying to spare you something that is at once empty and grandiose. But when I looked up I remember being able to see for the first time as far as one can see. There was truly nothing there, just a flatness that rolled away to the horizon, and the sky gaping like an open mouth. I walked with my head up, staring at the sky, until I heard Susan's voice. "John," she said, "look down." A last bit of yellow grass hung like thatch over a rift in the earth, and below that was the bare red clay of the cliff, dropping away from us at a steep angle. At its base a dry streambed whose flow had once been powerful enough to create this rift in the earth now wandered aimlessly, as if in search of its water. "There's only one way to do it," Susan said. She stepped off the edge and coasted on her ass in a cloud of red dust. I tried to step off carefully, but I was immediately lost in the cloud, the sound, the fall. Susan waited for me at the bottom. It seemed immensely warm down there and I looked up, searching for the wind, until I realized that it blew far above us now. I looked down. Susan's pants had red circles on the seat. "Did you bring a blanket?" she asked, and when she smiled her teeth were a reddish brown. Later, she screwed me with a passion and intensity that overwhelmed me: beneath her, I felt as useful as a newel post on a bed. I looked over her at the red wall of the cliff, at the invisible wall of the sky. Grit bit into my back: I hadn't brought a blanket. I remember thinking that I was some sort of freak because I felt no love, no lust even, no emotion for the girl straddling my hips. I remember thinking that I felt the same way about Susan that I did about my mother: I was trying to forget her while she was still there. And I remember trying to fit my father into it all, trying to blame him, and none of it worked, because these things had nothing to do with each other. I knew this, but not conflating them was impossible. Susan didn't say anything after I lost my erection, just dressed and led me from the prairie, and the land swallowed the cliffs behind us. As I followed her strong silent back I remember I felt that the night had somehow pushed its way inside me, and that I had been left in darkness.

On the night my mother finally died, while waiting in Penn Station for the train that would take me to the hospice, I met a man who made signs: the support columns of the platform had just been painted, and his signs read "blue wet-paint columns." One caught my eye just as I descended the stairs, as much for its odd syntax as its cheap handmade feel. I looked down the platform from one sign to the next and I was struck by the uniformity of them all. The handwriting was a sloppy scrawl of red marker, a mix of capital and lowercase letters that was repeated exactly from sign to sign.

My eye followed them down the platform until there were no more, and then I looked down and saw the sign maker, or his back anyway, a back as broad as a field. I walked to him slowly. The platform was deserted except for the two of us and a few mice gnawing candy wrappers between the tracks. When I reached him I stood silently behind him; a slight tension in his shoulders told me he was aware of my presence but he continued to work slowly, drawing his marker across the paper with his left hand and repeatedly glancing at a scrubby slip of paper held in his right. I knew without looking that the paper contained the words taped to the posts, and that they were written exactly as they were written on each sign. I cleared my throat and said, "Blue wet-paint columns." The man looked up. The details of his face were lost in a thick black beard, but I could see confusion in his eyes. A single sound erupted from his mouth like a burp: "Huh?" That's when I realized, suddenly and unexpectedly, that he couldn't read, that he was simply copying the words in his right hand as if they were drawings, stick figures dancing meaninglessly across the paper. "Blue wet-paint columns," I repeated, caught off guard, and I wondered then why I had approached him at all. His blank expression prompted me to point at the sign he was making, but I couldn't think what to say, so I read it yet again: "Blue wet-paint columns." Hadn't someone told him what he was writing? He examined the paper as if he'd never seen it before. "No," he said, "these're dry. It's the support posts that're wet." "No, your signs—" I started, but he interrupted me with a wave of his hand and stood up. "Don't tell me no, man. Those"—he pointed at the signs—"are dry. And these"—he pointed to a column —"are wet." He looked at me for a moment, and I thought I read a hint of fear in his eyes. He blinked suddenly, then walked to a column and smacked his palm against it, and then he slapped the hand on a sign. "Check it out," he said. "Wet." The imprint glistened under the heading "blue wet-paint columns" and I stared at it blankly for a moment. I tried again. "Look, it's just that your signs say—" "I *know* what they say," he cut me off again. "I been writing them all night. All night!" He raised his voice on the last words, and he raised his left hand as well, and then he shoved them both in my face. I started to dodge the blow, but his hand stopped a few inches from me and only then did I see red ink on his hand, smeared from heel to pinky. "I know what I'm writing," he said quietly. "I got the words under my skin." Under his skin, I thought. Like a disease, I thought, and then I remembered why I was in the station. It was always like that for me: just when I was trying to concentrate on one thing, something else came along and distracted me. The man's cheeks quivered just under his eyes: he was afraid, and I knew why. He realized I was aware of his lie, but that didn't bother him as much as the idea that I'd call him on it, that I'd cut through the story he'd been telling everyone, and probably himself. His sign, its bold handprint and lipstick letters, caught my eye. I looked at it for a moment, and then

I stepped backward. The man dropped his hand. "Aw, hey, man," he said, "I'm sorry, I'm really sorry, I didn't mean to—I'm sorry." I smiled, then I turned to leave. I didn't see any point in saying anything, but he called after me: "Hey, you can read them, can't you?" I looked back and nodded. "Yeah," I said, "I figured out what you meant."

Sometimes, alone in Kansas, I loved my father so much that I would push chairs against the walls lest he trip over one and crack his skull, and other times I hated him and I knew that, somehow, he was responsible for what had happened to my mother. On those days I stole things from his room —T-shirts, pens embossed with his company's name—and I destroyed them in the prairie. I never understood why I did this, because I didn't know how I felt about myself: every time I tried to think about myself I ended up thinking about them. I resented them, both of them, but especially my father's constant attempt to re-create my mother's presence in the house by wearing her apron, cooking her food, or using me as her stand-in. I began to deny his attempts to remember her, but each denial only prompted him to try harder. He took to coddling things she'd owned, an old blanket, a picture of her, a piece of jewelry she'd once worn. After he went to sleep I would take these objects to the attic and pack them in boxes, and seal the boxes tightly with tape. Eventually there were no more objects and he came for me. It was inevitable, I suppose; all these things had done was remind him of her, and what more tangible reminder existed than me? He followed me to my room one night, still wearing her apron, and when I sat on the bed he sat down heavily beside me. He stank of beer, and I tried to ignore him. I fell backward on the bed, and then I lifted my legs up and over him, and for an embarrassing moment I saw him in the V of my legs—I was coming from the shower and I had nothing on under my robe—and then I kicked my legs past him to the bed. I lay there rigidly, hands clenched in fists at my side. "John," he finally said, after saying many other things I don't remember, "you just don't know what I live with every day." But I did, I did know—or I knew at least that it had something to do with the way his hands kept pushing their way through my hair like a thick-toothed comb. "John," he said, "I'm sorry." But I wouldn't listen. Three words kept batting around my head until finally I let them out: "Don't touch me," I hissed, and my father's hand stopped automatically, like a machine, and then without speaking he left my room.

After my father's visit to my room it seemed that the only thing left was for me to visit his. I snuck in often and rifled through the papers in his night table: I wanted to find one thing, just one thing, that would at last confirm or disprove what I already knew. And so I came home one day, and hearing nothing, I wandered in. My father sat on his bed in a blue satin gown that clung to his waist and hips but sagged at the chest. A brown curly wig sat crookedly on his head, and the makeup on his face looked as though it had been applied following paint-by-numbers directions. I looked at him for a long time; he looked down at a red inch of lipstick poking from a silver capsule. Very slowly, the crayon-like tube twisted back into its chute. "It's not so easy to put this on," he said. "It's harder than it looks." Smears of red stole the shape of his mouth. His eyelids lowered, as if weighted by the globs of mascara sticking to them. He stood up, then nearly fell as his heels tipped out from under him. He removed his feet from the stretched-out shoes and turned his back to me. After a pause, he said, "Unzip me, please." I did it quickly, looking away when I saw the bra strap, and then I stepped far away from him. The straps fell off his shoulders loosely, and he carefully pushed the dress past his waist. "Your mother kept her figure better than I do, I guess." He wore her underwear, and the pale fabric stretched so tightly across his buttocks that I could see the split between them as if he were naked; red indentations marked the panties' outline after he took them off, and a few crumpled pieces of toilet paper fell to the floor when he took the bra off. There was a towel on the bed, and he wrapped it around his waist like men do before turning back to me. Catching sight of himself in the mirror, he stopped, pulled the wig off. "She had a shag once," he said, "and long hair came back in style, so she picked this up." He looked at it a moment then dropped it to the floor. My father the drag queen: his stage name, I suppose, would be Miss Communication. I moved farther out of his way than I had to as he passed me and went in the bathroom and closed the door behind him.

Sometimes my mind plays a trick on me, and I remember that as the last time I ever saw him. But I didn't leave home until a year later and he came out in just an hour, his lips still a little red, and he cooked dinner like he always did. Afterward he made his way to the shelf where he kept the liquor, and he poured himself a glass of whiskey which, as though it were bottomless, he never finished. If he did empty the bottle in our house he went to the pool hall, and on those nights I'd get a call at two in the morning from the bartender, asking me to come get my father. One time I found him at the bar's old piano, slumped on the keyboard. A ceramic cowboy on a rearing horse sat atop the piano, and as the bartender and I each grabbed an arm, my father stirred himself enough to say, "I never wanted anything that she didn't want." In the car, a little more sober: "She once told me that there was nowhere she could go where I wouldn't find her. She said she had to make *me* go away." And then he said, "She was my *wife*, dammit!"

I arrived at the hospice in the early hours of the morning; when the taxi I'd taken from the train station finally turned on the flagstone driveway I felt excited, as if I were visiting someone I hadn't heard from forever. I felt like I was going home too, for the hospice was only twenty miles from our old house. The main building was long and low, surrounded by scruffy pines. It reminded me of its patients: well scrubbed but decaying. The flagstones were hosed clean but cracked, the hedges trimmed but scraggly with age, the door freshly painted but the wood wasting away. And this is all there was to her life: long windowless hallways, a small room, a cane chair made for weightless bodies. It creaked under my weight. She sat there: they sponged her every day, combed her hair, brushed her teeth and gums with a piece of gauze wrapped around the wrong end of a toothbrush. She rolls her eyes, or perhaps it's just the muscles twitching. Her wandering eyes see a nurse's plump face, a picture of a lonely building lost in a field, her own wasted lap. I knew nothing about her save the things laid out for me: a bed so firm it seemed a person never slept in it; clothes years old yet like new; some pictures of my father and me, years out of date; and the letters she wrote me. No, not her, but someone with small handwriting who tucked a note in with the first letter. "I think I understand Bea when she speaks," this person wrote. "I read her everything, a sentence at a time, for her approval. I've not written anything against her wish. But I don't know if I've written everything she would have liked to say." Does that matter? I thought then of the man who couldn't read but still managed to write readable signs: he and this woman were both messengers with little idea of what they were sending or what would be received, and yet their indirect communication still managed to convey the most vital information. It was only there, sitting in the chair my mother sat in and reading about how she missed us—not me, *us*—that I was able to say, if only to myself, that he raped her. He raped her and he killed her. There was something he wanted—and I don't think it was just another child, a big family—there was something he wanted more than he wanted to believe that his wife could die if she became pregnant again, so he raped her. He didn't beat her, didn't rip her clothes off; chances are that all he did was hide her birth control pills or refuse to wear a condom, or however they took care of things in the years between my birth and my mother's second pregnancy. These facts settled around me, not with the surprise of discovery, but the familiarity of acknowledgment. But then, it was never really a question of clues but a simple matter of admitting something that I'd known for a long time; it was kind of like coming out.

Sometimes I feel that my mother is less a person than an idea in my head. But when I tell someone about her I'm always asked, Why'd she stay? Why'd she take it? and she becomes real again, a person. Like my father, like Susan, like any man I meet and sleep with once and never see again. I have to admit I don't know why she took it. And that's where this story stops, I think. That's where it fails. Of all the letters, only one is truly from my mother. Or is it really from me? It rested in a wrinkled envelope with a piece of string hanging out of it, a piece of string which, when pulled, pulled out a single letter, which goes round and round and round. No note came with the ring, but it, and the string which had held it around my mother's neck—all by themselves, they said everything.

He lives alone now, visited only by the person who cooks his meals. I will never see him again. I imagine him though, sitting in his old recliner. He holds the box I sent him, the box which, he knows, holds all that is left of his wife's life. A few articles of clothing, letters, a rubber band I found in a dresser entwined with some of her hairs. I imagine his hands, the same hands which held down my mother, which felt the mound of new life that grew beneath her skin, which brought spoonfuls of food to her mouth. They have withered, paled, the hairs on them are white now. He looks at them but he can't bring himself to use them to rip open the box. Instead he turns it over and over and listens to the soft rustle of things inside. I imagine him: in the silent living room of his empty house he sets the box down and reaches for his glass of whiskey, and as he drinks it I wonder if his thoughts are as divided as mine. Is it her that he's thinking of, or is it me?

THE BEGINNING OF
THE OCEAN

I

An old black pickup moves west on Sunrise highway. Something is loose in the bed, and it clanks loudly as the pickup races by. My parents ride in silence. He drives, she reads the pullout section of last week's Sunday paper. I occupy the seat of honor—perched between my father's legs, just behind the steering wheel and just before his stomach and chest. I hold his beer. I'm not supposed to let it spill, and I stare nervously at the sloshing liquid and will it to settle down. My gaze is so focused that when my father occasionally reaches for the beer, his huge, black-haired white hand seems like an intruder, and he has to smack my hands away when I cling too tightly. I am five years old.

Something's gone wrong. I don't understand yet, but people are talking about how summer refuses to end. It's November, but the air is still hot, and filled with the scent of overripe citrus. Hot dog vendors line the highway. They sit outside their vans, fanning themselves with wilted newspapers. Nobody knows what to do. At the beach, hurricane fencing bor-

ders the sand, but that's the only human element defining it. No beach chairs, no gaudy umbrellas, no people. I walk a few steps away from my parents and turn around and around, feeling, for the first time, how big it all is. I'm not sure whether that should frighten or excite me, and I stand on my tiptoes in the sand and look to see how they're taking it. My mother, shading her eyes from the world with her palm, says, "It's enough to make a body do things." My father just says a deserted beach is like being in your own home, and he drops his pants and puts on his swimsuit without even looking around. My mother opens her mouth again, but then she closes it without speaking.

Instead she snaps a sheet in the air, and white flashes: not just the sheet, but my mother's belly, and her swimsuit, and my father's butt. Then colors swirl in, mostly reds: my mother's hair, my father's chest and arms. He works construction these days, his sunburn comes from working outside without a shirt; my mother's hair color comes from a bottle. My suit's red too, from K mart. It's pale now, almost pink, but as soon as I splash into the water the color deepens, as if the water had refreshed the dye in the fabric.

It's my father's idea that we nap after we've been in the water for a while. "Naptime" is all he says, and then he sprawls on the middle of the blanket. Sighing, my mother sinks down to one side of him; she hasn't swum but only waded in ankle-deep, still reading her magazine and glancing up occasionally to look at me. I lie on the blanket, on the other side of my *father. He sighs now. It's different from my mother's sigh, contented. It registers his sense of balance: this is what a family looks like. I imagine I'm in an airplane overhead: looking down, I see the big mound of my father in the middle. The pale heap of my mother is on his right side, face and hair covered by a magazine. The small pile of me is on his left. I'm not as big as my mother yet, but my skin is tanned and my suit is wet and dark red, so I show up better on the sheet.*

I fall asleep quickly in the hot November sun, and at first I think the ocean invades my dreams, that high tide washes over my mind. But as I wake up gradually I realize it isn't the ocean I hear, it's loud breathing, and as I wake up more I realize that it's not mine but my father's. I open my eyes and without moving my head I can see his stomach, falling until ribs show, rising until it seems like a pregnant woman's. I try to sit up then, but without turning my father puts his left hand out and catches me in the stomach and pushes me back before I get halfway up. But I'm able to see over his stomach for a second, and in that second I see my father's other hand low on my mother's abdomen, and I see that the bottom of her swimsuit is pushed down as well.

After that I lie with my father's hand heavy on my stomach. I stare straight up and try to hear just the ocean, which is so loud, so clear with no people around. Still, I can't help but hear my father's breathing, and after a while I notice my mother's too, heavy like his, but faster, and—though I try not to—I can't help but picture her stomach fluttering under his right hand. His left hand claws my skin, but I know I have to stay quiet, so I bite my lip. I look down only once, and when I do I think I see my mother's fist pounding the base of my father's stomach, but just barely—you know how it is when you look at the sun for too long—and I immediately look up, but the sun burns my eyes and I close them.

Then I fall asleep again, and this time the water does invade my dreams. I'm swimming, diving down, looking for the beginning of the ocean, but soon I realize I've gone too far, I have to head for the surface or I'll run out of air. So I start swimming up, using my arms and legs, but even though the sun reflects off the water's surface just above me, I can't reach it, it seems to retreat from me. And just when it seems there isn't any air left in my lungs, that I will drown, my eyes open and I feel my father's hand pressing down so hard on my stomach that I can't breathe. Then, just as I start squirming, my father's hand flies up and he groans loudly. And I want to cry out too, but all I can do is cry in, as I suck, vainly, at all the air that his hand has forced out of me; and then, as I hear the sound of labored breathing coming from the far side of his body, something comes to me from my dream, some half-human shape crawls out of the dark water, and I realize that my father has been drowning my mother as well.

D R I F T W O O D

∎

My father hid in the forest's shadow with his shotgun. It was twilight, and the evening was further darkened by thousands of crows clotting the sky. Lying in the hammock on the back porch, I could just make out the gun looped through my father's right arm. His head was tilted back; I didn't think he could see me. All at once he raised the shotgun and fired once, twice, six times in all, and the crows, whose calls had been loud, started to shriek. Several dark shapes fell to the ground and the dogs ran toward them. My father laughed and a rain of excess pellets shredded the forest's leaves. Snarling, the dogs fought over the carcasses.

The crows were gone the next morning except for scattered feathers. Major, one of my father's German shorthairs, looked at me wearily, then returned to the mangled paw he'd been licking ever since it had been ruined by one of my father's traps two years before. Squire, his replacement, got up, vomited, then followed me to the old barn. The night before, as dinner ended, my father said, "The dogs'll probably be sick in the morning. Make sure they have plenty of fresh water and give them this leftover liver—and stop picking that thing." My hand fell from my face, where it had been tracing the crescent-shaped scar that curls around my right eye. I pushed my chair back and started to leave, then waited by the door when I heard my mother sigh at the sink, where she was washing dishes. "Don't worry him, Henry," she said. "How would you like being scarred for life?" Her voice stopped when she noticed me still in the room. Without looking at me, my father sighed also, a wheeze like a punctured tire, and then he pushed past me and went to bed. Now, in the morning, Squire followed me so closely that he tripped on my heels. "Get lost, you mutt," I yelled. He backed away a few steps, looked at me blankly. One of my father's coffee cups sat on a fencepost, and I grabbed it and threw it at Squire. It missed and cracked loudly on the driveway gravel. I looked up at the house's gray windows to see if anyone had heard, but the windows returned my stare as blankly as Squire did, and told me nothing.

The old barn seemed to list in a breeze as I walked to it. We'd named it the old barn when my father started talking of building a new one, just before my older brother drowned. Inside, the heat was like July, not mid-September, and dust motes clogging the hundred-degree air were made iridescent by streams of light poking through holes where Justin had pulled a few planks from the roof. The stench of The Glue

Factory's shit hit me, and I started breathing through my mouth. I couldn't remember the last time her stall had been raked clean. Squire trotted in behind me, sprayed a fencepost, started sniffing at the ladder leading to the loft. "What's up, Lassie?" I said. My father hated it when I called Squire Lassie. The dog ignored me; he whined nervously, then stretched his paws up the ladder and barked. Though Squire barked at the loft every other day and I knew it was probably just a rat or a cat, I needed an excuse not to clean The Glue Factory's stall. I pushed Squire out of the way and went up. A few bales of hay, a layer of loose straw, a pile of dented unmarked boxes: that's all I saw when my head poked through the loft floor. Then I climbed another step and saw him. A boy. He stared at me where I perched on the ladder staring at him. His eyes were bleary, and a clump of straw stuck to the left side of his face. He looked about my age, sixteen or so. I was sixteen, I mean. He was or so.

"Who are you?"

Something happened then. Though I'd spoken, I realized as soon as my mouth opened that the same question must be on his mind, and for just a second I became him, saw out of his eyes, looked through a veil of straw at a boy with an eye encircled by a pale scar that sliced through his tan. But then, before I could evaluate what I saw, I was back inside myself, looking out. As I watched, the boy glanced around the loft. I imagined he was looking for an escape route. Turning back to me, he swallowed. "Have you ever ridden in a limousine?" "What?" I said, startled, "I've never even seen one." "Have you ever looked at the world from the top of a sixty-story building?" I didn't understand his game, but I tried to play. "I've climbed the cottonwood in the front yard. Does that count?" I smiled hopefully. "Have you ever fucked?" I looked down, embarrassed. "No." I heard another loud swallow. "I'm hungry." "My mother will be cooking soon," I told him. "Want to eat with us?" He just stared past me with unfocused eyes. I climbed into the loft. "Come on," I said, looking at the straw all over him. "Let's brush this off and get going." His eyes met mine suddenly, and he put a hot finger on my scar. I jerked back. "The Glue Factory," I said. "Our horse." "Your horse?" "Kicked me," I said, and added, "We'd better hurry." I brushed at the straw on his face. "I'll tell my mother you're a friend from school." The straw stuck to his skin so I grabbed some and pulled it free. One second there was nothing; the next, a thick red line of blood ran from his eyebrow to his chin, closing fast on the buttoned collar of his white shirt. Without a sound, he fell backward in the hay, and the sun coming through the holes Justin had left behind made zebra stripes of light and shadow on his body.

I'm trying to tell it the way he would: one minute he's in a barn, a stranger picking at his face, the next he's in a bed; the skin of his face tingles and a stiff bandage covers his eye. His shirt is gone. He smells, close by, soap, and farther away, food: toast, eggs, frying bacon. Then a big fussy woman dressed in a man's work clothes enters the room with a platter. "Here now," she says. "I'm Bea. Don't try to talk yet. Just eat, and I'll be back for the tray in a bit." I think I know how he felt: I remember waking in the hospital, and the first thing I saw with my uncovered eye was an ugly shirt patterned with blue flowers. I tried to remove it, wondering vaguely where my T-shirt was, but my eye started to hurt and I became tired. When I awoke the second time, I remember, the hospital gown seemed familiar.

The kitchen table and a coffee cup separated my father from me. Dressed for work in stained jeans and a T-shirt distended over his stomach, he held his coffee at arm's length. "You just found him there?" he asked, addressing the cup. "Yeah. Squire was nosing around the ladder, so I checked it out." He tapped his cup, and the coffee rippled with waves. "He say anything? His name, where he's from, anything like that?" "Nothing." The phone rang and my mother answered it. Then, pressing the receiver to her chest, she said, "It's Mr. Johnson. He wants to know—" "Tell him I'm on my way," my father said, and started for the door with his coffee. As my mother hung up, he told her, "We'll discuss this more tonight. For now, just keep an eye on him. And you"—he pointed to me. "Finish your chores before you're late for school, and don't skip out on The Factory's stall." He stepped outside and the screen door banged shut. My mother was at the sink by that time; she stopped washing dishes for a moment and rested her weight on her elbows. Pausing on the top step, my father looked into his cup. "Squire was sniffing around there, huh?" "Yeah." He sipped from his cup. "Damn good dog," he said, and then he walked to his truck, climbed in, and drove away.

When my father entered the house that evening, the screen door announced his arrival just as it had his departure, and his voice was like a second slam. "Bea!" he hollered. Drying her hands on her pants, my mother bustled in from the bathroom. I slipped in behind her. I'd eaten earlier and had no reason to be in the kitchen, but the door's sound reeled me in like a fish. "Quiet," my mother said. "You'll wake Martin." My father grabbed a beer from the fridge and snapped it open. "Martin," he said, his voice only slightly quieter. "John tell you his name?" "No, Martin did " My mother set a plate at my father's place and hastily arranged the silverware around it. "You get his last name?" my father said, sitting down and picking up his fork. "Just let me stir this up a little and it'll be ready to go," my mother said from the stove. She worked a spoon into the stew we'd eaten for dinner, then pulled four biscuits from the oven. "They got a little hard," she said. "Sorry." She ladled three huge dollops on my father's plate and crowded the biscuits around. "He didn't tell me his last name." My father harrumphed. "No one at the pool hall knew anything about a runaway or a lost kid," he said, already eating. He stuffed his mouth, chewing only once or twice before swallowing. "You want something besides that?" my mother asked, wiping her dry hands on a towel. My father swigged his beer. "This is doing me just fine." My mother pulled a glass from the cabinet, set it on the table, and emptied the can into it. It clinked as she tossed it with the other aluminum under the sink. "John honey," she said, still bent over, facing the cabinet. "This box is almost full here. Are you going to empty it sometime soon?" I didn't look at her. "I had a busy day," I said. "Nope, no one's heard of a Mar-tin at all." My father broke the word in half as if sounding it out, then forked another bite of stew. My mother set a small plate and fork in front of me. Her fingers tapped the table once, and I looked up and met her gaze, and then my eyes darted between her and my father several times, and then I just stared at my plate until she turned away.

"That Johnson," my father was saying, pushing his empty plate away and reaching for his beer. "Do you know how much he got for plumbing that new Casa del Sol?" I looked at him over my mother's arm as she placed a thick slice of chocolate cake in front of me. I shook my head; my father drank some beer. "Let me tell you: thirty thousand dollars." I widened my eyes as far as I could, my mouth already full of cake. "More?" my mother said, a hand on his plate. "I'm full, thank you very much," he said, and my mother moved to the oven and played with the towel in her hands. To me, my father said, "And who *really* did that restaurant?" "You," I got out between bites. "Damn straight I did." My father shoved his chair back several feet, almost hitting my mother "That little Mex just wrote out the check like it was nothing. Here you are, Señor Mister Johnson sir, and thank you very much. Well," my father said, and then he swigged the last of his beer and set his glass on the table heavily, "I guess I'll be damned if I'll ever see money like that." As he walked from the kitchen my mother swept his plate and glass from the table. He stopped in the doorway and turned on me. "You clean The Factory's stall today?" My jaw stopped working and a forkful of cake clung to the roof of my mouth like wet clay. I stared at my father. He looked back, one hand rubbing the expanse of his belly. "Well?" "Henry, please," my mother said. "John always does his chores." "Well then," my father said. "Good night, *family*." My mother watched me while I chewed and swallowed the last bite of cake. Behind his closed door, my father burped. The sound was short and explosive, but muffled, like a distant gunshot. I put my fork and plate in my mother's outstretched hand. She kissed me on the forehead. "I've made up the couch for you tonight," she said. Her voice was tired. I wanted to apologize for not taking out the cans, but I didn't. As I left the kitchen I heard her behind me, washing away the last traces of the meal.

Waking up during the night put me back in the hospital: the living room walls weren't what I normally opened my eyes to, and the strange pull of pajamas had me scratching my neck and crotch. I sat up just in time to see the refrigerator

.ght go off. After a few seconds I heard a glass being set on the metal grate in the sink. I slid down into the couch and watched my father walk past the door, feet heavy on the linoleum. A few minutes later I walked as silently as I could to my room. Hearing nothing, I moved to my parents' door; it was partially open, but I couldn't make out the bed. My father was already snoring. Back on the couch it was hot and the blanket weighed on my body, but I didn't kick it off. In the hallway the clock cuckooed three times. Then, almost as if he'd heard, our stupid rooster crowed, announcing a dawn still hours away.

At school, kids I hardly knew asked me questions that started with "My father told me. . . ." I told them nothing. They'd been like that the day after Justin's funeral, and when I told them about Justin they just nodded their heads solemnly—they didn't understand. Because it wasn't solemnity I felt, it was just a strangeness. And telling them, or telling my teachers, who gave me breaks on my tests as though my brain were dead and not my brother, just made me feel empty. Robbed, really, of a feeling that I hadn't even had time to understand. No, Martin was mine, and I told them nothing about him, nothing at all.

By the time I got home it was four o'clock. There was still an hour or more before my father came in. I found my mother on the living room couch, her sewing baskets filling the cushions on both sides of her. I sat down, resting my back against the foot of the couch and her soft leg. "How was school?" she asked. "Fine," I said. "Everyone was talking about Martin." "Word travels fast." She chuckled a bit, and I heard the nearly silent rasp of thread being pulled through fabric. "What did you do today?" I asked her. "Well, I'll tell you," my mother said, and her finger tapped me on the head once. "I was going out by the old barn to see how much firewood we have, and I nearly stepped on a rattlesnake." "No!" "Really, John, I'm serious." "But I didn't think there were any around here. I thought the woods were too cold for them." "They don't come from the woods, they come from the fields. An old barn is a great place for them to catch rats and mice, not to mention poach eggs." She worked another length of thread through whatever it was she was sewing. "So what did you do?" I asked. "You mean after I pulled my heart out of my mouth? Well, I went straight for your .22. And then I thought, The dogs, and I called them in. You can just imagine. Squire was flipping cartwheels at being let in the house, and Major just limped straight to your father's chair and went to sleep." I laughed with her, looking at my father's big brown chair, and imagined Major curled in its sunken seat. "Well, Martin practically jumped out of bed when I barged into your room. And he nearly had a heart attack when I grabbed your gun from the closet. Snake, I said, though I doubt that made him feel any better, but I was gone before he could say anything." She laughed. "I think I interrupted him, you know?" Quickly I said, "You shot it." "One shot, through the head. Surprising even my-self, I might add." I turned and looked up at her. "You're not putting me on, are you?" She dropped her needle and thread noisily and raised her arms in an open gesture. "Have I ever put you on before?" "No," I had to admit, and turned around again. A moment later, I heard a thread snap. "So what did Martin do today?" "Stayed in bed. I think his eye is bothering him more than he lets on." She seemed about to go on, but just then the dogs barked and pebbles crunched in the driveway. "Is that your father already?" my mother asked, and her sewing supplies rattled as she stuffed them in a basket. "Well, isn't he early today?" I followed her to the kitchen, surprised when, moments later, Martin joined me at the table. He wore the jeans I'd found him in and one of my shirts. "Well, look who's up," my mother said, stopping what she was doing to wash her hands and pour Martin a glass of milk. "How's your eye feeling?" "Fine," he said, lightly touching the bandage. "Thanks for the milk." "Oh, nothing at all," my mother said, and stopped for a moment to look at Martin. "Nothing at all." Martin looked into his glass of milk, but he didn't drink it.

My father opened the door. He stood in it long enough to pat a couple of panting brown snouts and then he entered the house, the door slamming on the heels of his boots. "We're having pork chops," my mother announced. "Hi, son," my father said, but he wasn't looking at me. Martin looked up from his milk. "You're Henry, right?" "I'm

Henry," my father said. "John tell you that?" "No, Bea did."
From the counter my mother said, "Mr. and Mrs. seemed
so stuffy—" "You," my father interrupted her, turning to
me. "What is your rifle doing by the old barn?" Wide-eyed,
I looked from my father to my mother. The last hour vanished
from my brain. I extended my hand, pointing at my mother.
"It was her," I said, "she did it." "That true?" my father said,
no longer looking at me. My mother laughed a little. "Oh,
I completely forgot about it. The excitement of the moment,
I guess." "What *are* you talking about?" My father came the
rest of the way into the kitchen, went to the refrigerator,
popped open a beer. "You'll never believe it," she said, back
to him, hands buried in a bowl of something. "There was a
rattlesnake out there. Four feet long, I'd guess." "Horseshit,"
my father said. "There aren't any rattlers around here. Stop
making excuses." He sat at the table across from Martin,
adjacent to me. Quietly, my mother said, "Well, I'm pretty
sure it was a rattlesnake." "Horseshit," my father said again.
"Female hysteria. And it's still no excuse for leaving a gun
lying around where anyone, one of the dogs, anything, might
happen across it." In a solemn voice he added, "You know,
after what happened with Justin I'd have thought you'd be a
little more responsible." My mother washed her hands again,
then went to her baking cabinet. She returned with a plate
of brownies and set them heavily on the table. "Here," she
said. "Dinner won't be ready for an hour. Might as well help
yourself." To my father she said, "It won't happen again."

Suddenly I was behind Martin's eyes again, and the bandage over the left one gained new meaning. Half a picture, it must seem like. *What happened here?* I'd have asked myself if I were he: where's the other half? Martin raised his milk to his mouth and drained the glass in one quick movement. I waited impatiently for him to ask his question, for my parents to try to answer it. But all he said was, "Need any help?" He spoke to my mother. My father laughed as if he'd just heard an absurd joke, then grabbed the brownies. "Make these in between shooting rattlers?" he said. "Or bears?" He laughed again, then left the room. Loudly, I said, "I told her I didn't believe her." Martin looked up at me. He seemed confused, but he turned away when my mother put her hand on his shoulder. "Why don't you join John and his father in the living room and watch a little TV or something while I finish dinner?" She picked up his glass. Her cheeks were red, her forehead damp. Then she reached her empty hand in her pants pocket and pulled out something. She fingered it once or twice noisily, then set it before me. "This is for you," she said, and went back to the sink. The object on the table was semi-transparent. Its thirteen beads were irregularly shaped, and it was pierced at the top by a braided length of dark blue thread. I slid it off the table as quietly as possible, but the beads announced themselves with each motion. Then, the rattle silenced in my pocket, I went to the living room. My father was wiping the chair seat and his backside. "Goddammit," he said. "Dog hair everywhere."

*   *   *

Martin slept quietly, though his body seemed incredibly hot. Maybe I just wasn't used to anyone sleeping beside me. My father's only comment about Martin's continued presence was that he wasn't going to have someone sleeping on his couch every night. Every half hour or so, Martin rearranged himself, arms, legs, which side he slept on. Once, he twisted about in bed, and when he'd finished one of his arms lay across my stomach. Crickets ground their legs together among the closed petals of the roses struggling on that side of the house. I could feel a line of sweat forming underneath Martin's arm. He coughed once, then started snoring quietly. I tapped the rattle I'd tied to my neck and suddenly both he and the crickets were silent.

My mother took the bandage off Martin's face on a Wednesday, and all day Thursday I stared at the long curved scab that just chopped off his left eyebrow. By Friday I was used to it, just as I'd become accustomed to sleeping under his arm. On Saturday, as we were waking, I said, "Want to go for a walk?" Martin pulled his arm from my body and rolled across the bed. "Where?" he said, sounding wide awake and wary already; I was still half-asleep and hadn't thought about the question before asking it. "Swimming," I said. This, too, just popped out. "So you mean, do I want to go swimming?" "Well, it's a long walk there." Martin jumped from bed. His tan legs and a yellow T-shirt, one of mine, made his underwear seem even more white. He grabbed a red shirt from the floor, a button-down, and put it on over the T-shirt. "Sure," he said then, pulling on a pair of blue jeans. In the living room, my mother vacuumed underneath my father's propped-up legs. His mouth was distended over a BLT and he watched a television made silent by the vacuum's roar. My mother looked up as we walked by, still pushing the vacuum back and forth. "Where are you off to?" she called. "We're going for a walk," I said. "We're going swimming," Martin said at the same time. "What?" my mother said, her face confused. "Walking," I said, and showed her with my hand, index and middle fingers striding an imaginary path. "Swimming," Martin said, and pantomimed the act, one arm over the other. "What!" my mother yelled, her eyes wide and darting from me to Martin. My father pushed her out of the way of the TV with his leg. He yelled over the vacuum, "Get. But don't forget your chores." Quickly I pushed Martin outside, and my mother's final protest—"But they didn't eat"—was cut off by the closing door.

The sound of an approaching car overtook us on the road. When Martin heard it, he stopped. He turned and looked at the car, and when it got a little closer he pushed me back a foot so he could see it, and be seen by it, clearly. I started to ask him what was up, but he cut me off. "Just try to disappear for a sec, okay?" When the car was about fifty feet away, he posed himself. There's no other word for it. He stood with his legs spread wide, pants pulled up tight in the crotch, pelvis pushed forward. His shoulders were thrown back and the button-down rode low on them, flapping like a cape, and with his right hand he pushed up his T-shirt so that a taut line of bare stomach was exposed. At the last minute, he pushed his bangs over his left eye. The car was big and old and rust-eaten, and it came up on us fast, and then, I'm not sure, but I think it was just as Martin pulled up his shirt, it slowed down with a short screech of dry brake pads, and at the sound I was moved as I had been so many times in the past few days behind another person's eyes, this time the eyes of the old man driving the car. And there was Martin: he looked like a— I was going to say he looked like a prostitute, but who ever heard of a boy prostitute? And there I was: head down, hands in pockets, looking like— The car suddenly sped up and passed us in a cloud of dust. When it disappeared over a slope Martin started walking again. "What was that?" I asked. "An experiment." "Did it succeed or fail?" "Both," Martin said, and though I didn't feel he'd told me anything really, the way he said it made me decide not to ask another question.

Then we were tramping across the fields, my feet sweating inside my boots. Martin looked more comfortable in my sneakers. He'd been wearing penny loafers when I found him, but they're useless for trekking. Eventually the land grew boggy and started to sink in on itself and I said, "We're almost there." In the distance a darker spot of brown gradually revealed itself to be a small pond. The pond was surrounded by a long lazy half-moon of limestone, a twenty-foot-high strip pocked by small black caves that glowed white in the distance and served as a narrow border between the brown grass and the blue sky. But it was the pond in the center of this canyon that held my eye. Coffee-colored, it bristled at the edges with tangled junipers and the muddy imprints of animal tracks. A light breeze across its surface gave the illusion of waves. "It's a puddle," Martin said. "You swim in that?" "We used to all the time. I haven't been for two years." "Well, I guess we're here now." Martin took his clothes off, slung them on a bush. Taking slow steps, he minced his way to the pond, stopped in the muck at the water's edge. "Ugh. This is like walking in diarrhea." "Isn't it great?" I said. All the sudden I felt happy, happy to finally be here again. I had my clothes off and tried not to fall on my way to the pond. Martin bent over, picked up a handful of mud, flung it at me. The mud struck my chest, but it was the rattle's sound that made me laugh nervously, not the sticky mass splatting on my skin. "Darling," Martin said, and his eye had a strange, faraway glow. I thought for a moment that he was calling me darling, and I blushed. Then he spoke again: "It's just darling," he said, and my blush cooled as though a chilly wind had blown across my skin.

Hours later, under a juniper tree. A residue of brown silt on both our naked bodies, Martin leaning into my stomach. Short muddy lines on his back where his hair dripped, water collecting in the crease where our bodies met. The pond was still, as though no one had ever disturbed it. Martin's voice: I wasn't looking at him and it seemed to come from the air, the pond, my own mind. "This is where he drowned, isn't it?" "Sshh," I whispered, "look over there." A deer, a small long-eared doe, stood at the pond's far edge. "Ooh," Martin breathed. Slowly the deer lowered her head. Without thinking, I tapped the rattles suspended from my neck. The deer's head shot up. Martin turned to me, the scab dominating his face. He shook the rattle, and the deer's head twisted from side to side, and mine did too, but Martin saw only me. I put my hand over his. "Don't," I whispered, but too late: the deer leapt away, white tail flashing in the twilight. I closed my eyes for a moment, but when I opened them Martin was still there, and he continued to look at me expectantly. There was too much knowledge in his eyes, too much *story*. "Yes," I finally said, and his right eye blinked. "Yes, this is where he drowned." And then I was up, grabbing my clothes, finding my shoes, and, not dressing, carrying my things pressed to my chest to keep the rattle quiet, I ran away like the deer.

My father, a know-nothing about horses, handed me my mother's paring knife and said, Trim her tail. Her coat was softened by age and she was bald over her shoulders. Her tail was tangled, full of burrs, and standing behind her, face turned from the farts she let out every five minutes, I sawed through coarse thick hairs. I felt the knife jab her skin, and the next thing I knew was waking in the hospital, and everything had changed. My head was swimming and Justin had been dead for months. My parents sat at the foot of my bed. My father was weeping, my mother had pulled her long dress into her lap. Suddenly my father was on top of her, straddling her, his hand around her throat. Your fault! he hissed. It's all your fault! He smacked her face back and forth with his free hand. She tried to speak, but couldn't. I tried to speak, but couldn't. It was like he was choking both of us. That's when I closed my eyes. That's when I closed my eyes, and I prayed that when I opened them he would be gone. But when I opened them he was still there and my mother's neck was ringed with a collar of purple and black bruises, and we all looked at each other, but no one said anything.

"I thought I'd find you here." Darkness was punctuated by an even blacker shadow, and straw rustled as it crossed the stall. There was another, indeterminate sound, low, raspy as well. The Glue Factory murmured in her sleep, and then a brief spurt of laughter played through the still air. "Your parents think you drowned." "What? Why?" "Didn't you hear them tear out of here?" "I was sleeping." "When I showed up your old man had me by the shoulders, shook me like a doll. Where's John? Where's John? he kept saying." For the first time he actually touched me: grabbed me, shook. That noise again. "Hey, where's your shirt?" "I was hot." He pushed away from me silently. A few feet away The Glue Factory pawed the straw. I felt him waiting. "Accidents don't just happen, you know," I said. "Why not?" "People don't just drown in three feet of water. There's got to be a reason. It's got to be someone's fault." "So what happened?" "He drowned." "What *really* happened?" "I fell asleep and he drowned, dammit! I was supposed to be watching him and I fell asleep and he drowned! And my father said it was her fault and, and that's how we've lived ever since." Sitting back, I felt the individual slats of wood press against my back and I heard that noise again. I realized then that it accompanied me, as though at some point—when he questioned me, when I answered, or perhaps just when he touched me—he had transferred a part of himself to me. "I'm sorry," he said. "I won't talk about it anymore." He leaned forward in the straw and put his hand on my chest. "I won't talk anymore." There was no reason for his touch, no meaning, and his fingers wandered aimlessly across my torso. He kissed me. "Stop," I said. "The horse will see." "Sshh," Martin whispered. "We're on her blind side."

For a moment I accepted everything. I accepted it because he had, and still he'd kissed me. Sudden relief filled my body, and I started laughing, a deep laugh that rumbled out of my chest and burst into the stall with a powerful extra dimension of sound. The Glue Factory lurched awake and started shuffling around, but I hardly noticed. Still laughing, I pulled my legs to my chest to avoid her hooves. "John—" The Glue Factory's hoof crashed against the wall. Martin and I stood simultaneously, and that's when I pinpointed the sound.

"John," Martin repeated. "The rattle." "I know, I know." "Take it off. Get rid of it, quick." I pulled at it, which only made it shake louder. "It's tied too tight. We've just got to get out of here." The Glue Factory lashed out again, her hoof striking the wood hard enough to crack it. We vaulted the wall just before she crashed against it. I grabbed Martin's hand and we ran outside. Outside, I laughed again, loud this time, louder than the rattle which bounced off my chest. I stopped when I heard my name. "John." It was Martin. He looked at me in the moonlight but he didn't say anything else. Quietly I said, "Let's go inside. Let's go to bed," and Martin's sigh seemed less relieved than resigned. I remember finding his scab in the darkness with my hand. "Who did this?" I asked. Martin laughed, and his laugh frightened me more than the rattle's rattle. "Someone I loved for a little while," he said, pushing my fingers away. In the morning, I reached to pull his arm across my body, but it wasn't there. He wasn't there. He'd gone.

We only really met in little ways: a line of sweat, muddy trails of water, a traced scab, a kiss. My mother cooked him food, my father tried to boss him around. I don't think we were ever quite aware of how we depended on him, but he filled a space in our lives, the space created by Justin's death. That's obvious. But we labored for too long under the idea that we knew him better than he knew us, when all we really knew was what we wanted him to be. So in the morning, when he was gone, the house seemed incredibly vacant, and we realized that we didn't know what had left it this time, nor what to use to fill the space left behind. Here it is now: a brown thing, long and rectangular, a little white on the bottom. In the back is the forest, filled with evening shadows and nesting crows. In the front the empty field stretches past our fence to the horizon. My father sits on the tailgate of his truck, cleaning my rifle in the half-light. I can just make out my mother hanging clothes up to dry. I've turned the whole thing over and over in my mind, worked at it the way the water worked at the piece of driftwood I found wrapped in my parents' muddy clothes this morning. How long did it take before the water seeped in, how long before the wood split and revealed its secrets? I could look into it now if I wanted to, but instead I'm taking it to the pond so it can float back where it came from. It may seem like I'm walking away, but I'll be back soon. I'll be back for dinner. There's no point in looking too deep. Because if you stare too hard into the open veins of a piece of driftwood, eventually you'll see that all the dark places reveal is more wood.

GIVEN THIS AND
EVERYTHING

I

People think my arm's hurt, but it's not. Just my fingers. I hold myself this way so people can't see them. Better they think my arm's hurt than see what my fingers look like.

I tell them it's not my father's fault my fingers don't go straight. At school, they call ours a broken home. I used to think they meant the kitchen faucet, which dripped. But they meant my mother.

David, who calls himself my friend, advises me: Keep the kitchen clean. Keep the radio down. Keep out of his way. But he doesn't know much, what with two parents and plumbing that works.

What happened was: I waited too long. Didn't tell anyone. I hid the red ball of my hand in a pocket. It hurt so bad I limped. It sounded like a rattle shaken under water. Then I passed out. I woke up in the hospital. I thought, He knows.

At first even he blamed himself. He said, I was full of beer, my mind was empty, I didn't know what I was doing. Doesn't that prove his innocence?

Since my mother, my father piles brown-bagged groceries on the table. He says putting them in cabinets is just an extra step to clutter up his mind. When he cooks for us, the stuff goes straight from the table into a pot, then back to the table.

Meat and milk and things like that, beer, he still keeps in the fridge.

Empties go in a box under the sink.

He pees every morning after he gets up, like clockwork. I hear him through the wall. He sounds like a waterfall. I know from peeing with him that he covers the bowl with bubbling foam. Compared to me, it's a flood. Compared to David—ha!

David says, Maybe you should offer to take his boots off for him—David still blames my father. But he didn't even know us then. And what's he know now? Just what happened. Not how.

I thought I'd fix the faucet, see, impress him. You might think he'd have fixed it, but he's got things on his mind. And I'd seen him work, I thought I knew what to do. But I'd only managed to pull things apart when he came in. The radio was loud, the kitchen a soggy mess, I didn't hear his boots on the linoleum. He stepped on my hand, hard.

Afterward he made me mop it up. And don't think I'm selfless or anything: I held that against him. But still, I hid my hand from him. How could he have known what he'd done?

My father wanted me to play baseball. He gave me a mitt

once. He gives me this, and everything. Sometimes I dream he throws me balls, but since I can't catch them with my hand (I was right-handed) I use my teeth.

And you might think, given this and everything, that I would love him less. But it's just us two. And when he's drunk, it's like me and half of him. Or maybe twice him, I don't know.

Even he doesn't understand. He says, I don't know why you love me. I want to say, I don't know why you hurt me, but I'm afraid that would make him angry. So I just laugh instead.

Before, enough water dripped from the faucet to fill the spaghetti pot every fifteen minutes. I was kept busy, emptying it. You might think I could've just let it drip down the drain, but without measuring things how can you say what you've lost?

The faucet stopped dripping after my father fixed it. But it doesn't get hot water now. I don't think that has anything to do with the faucet, more with something deeper, inside our house. But my father doesn't know this—he needs me to tell him. And me? I need him to fix it. I already know I can't do it alone.

T R A N S F O R M A T I O N S

I

Something flickered in the darkness. The light, a tiny, hand-held candle, wavered for a moment, then danced about like a firefly. Its illumination was too ephemeral to really be called light: it was a pallor, a skin-tone glow of marble whiteness. The sheets on the bed were white as well, crisp underneath with hospital corners and turned back on top at the perfect forty-five-degree angle. We drew in a breath, and then, with a sigh less an exhalation than a movement, slipped into the sheets, the down of our bodies ruffled by their cotton coolness. The faint smell of bleach raised the hair on the napes of our necks. With blind hands and animal instinct we made love, the candle glowing white somewhere behind us, the sheets yellowing with sweat like soft butter around our thighs, a blue night just visible at the edge of the curtain. We moved quickly, slowly, not at all; there might have been some blood, blotting rose petals on the sheet, but no pain. Then, sleeping, it was over; the sun rose behind our eyelids and washed out the room, and everything in it became translucent. Looking in, anyone could have seen us and felt our bodies pressed together under the blanket and known what we had done; my face on his chest, our breathing synchronous, rose and fell like a wine cork on the waves.

It should have been like that: lights, camera, action, everything. Heavy on the filters, a little fog drifting in from under the bed. But I lost my virginity to my stepfather on my mother's double bed during the afternoon's heat while she was at work. Salty water rolled off our bodies and the bed creaked under our weight like old bones; it was far too hot to climb between the sheets. He wouldn't look at me while we did it, and he was quick about his business. Afterward, we sat in bed and he held me, staring blankly at the door and occasionally running his fingers through my hair as he'd done for the past two months, ever since he'd started sleeping with my mother. They weren't married at the time we had sex, not even engaged, and I was pretty sure he was the first man since my father's death a year and a half before. He'd had cancer. Liver, spleen, stomach, intestine. Just about all his guts rotted away.

My mother had come home from the hospital the day he died—he'd been in six months—and I knew what had happened because she was in the kitchen smoking a cigarette and drinking a rum-and-Coke when I came home from school. The knob on the front door nearly came off in my hand as I entered the trailer; it had broken more than a week before.

My mother didn't really greet me when I walked through the door, just called out, "Come on in here." Her words weren't slurred, but they came out in two uneven bursts. I walked in the kitchen and sat down at the table. A package of Kents lay on the table, a few of the cigarettes scattered about like the crooked spokes of a bicycle tire, and two open bottles—a plastic one, half filled with Coke, and a glass one, nearly emptied of Captain Morgan's Spiced Rum—were on the table next to her. She'd pushed the placemat away, and the formica tabletop was scarred with scattered water rings near where she sat, as if she'd been not just drinking but moving the glass around for hours. She didn't say anything so I unpacked my lunch box, pulling out the empty sandwich bag, apple core, and half a Twinkie, and set them all on the table. My thermos sloshed when I lifted it, and I remembered that I hadn't drunk it all at lunch that day. I unscrewed the lid cup and the inner plug, and filled the cup with flat pop. Then we sat at the table for a few minutes, each of us drinking and refilling our cups, me with just Coke, she with Coke and the last of the rum. "So," she said finally. "It's over." I nodded my head; I knew that. "Okay?" she asked me. What did she mean, okay? Was it okay with me that my father was dead? Was I okay? "He's dead," I said. "Yeah, he's dead," she said, and started crying. "Oh, my baby," she said through her tears, and I didn't know if she meant me or him. She came over and squeezed herself in the chair with me, wrapped both arms around my shoulders, and shook me with her sobs.

Then I started crying too and soon the tears rolled off my nose and cheeks and splashed in the forgotten cup I half held in my lap.

We'd been expecting his death for a while but still we cried a lot. Too much, perhaps: for two or three days we didn't stop. We were new there, and we had no relatives within a thousand miles, nor any close friends in town. With no one to share our grief and measure it out, we expended it in one great, incomplete burst of tears, and it seemed we stopped feeling when we couldn't cry anymore. Later, she'd sometimes ask me to be with her until she fell asleep. "Come stay with me," she'd say, always waiting until I'd gotten ready for bed. I'd just go to the door at first and stand there to see if perhaps she'd already passed out. There was always a glass beside her bed; on bad nights there were the rum and Coke bottles as well. "Come right here," she'd say if she was still awake, and pat the side of her bed. I would go over and kneel beside her, facing the picture of my father on her bed table. In the winter I'd be in my pajamas, in the summer just a T-shirt and underwear. I can still taste the toothpaste, feel my face tingling from the washcloth, see in the glass protecting my father's picture my own hair, damp and combed straight back. The long ends tickled my shoulders and dripped water down my back. My mother would put one hand on my father's empty space beside her, the other on my head, and leave them there except for when she needed a drink. Then her hand kind of slid off my head to the table and grabbed the glass. At some point she usually knocked over my father's picture, and during the course of a night, each time her hand returned to my head it fell a little harder: a tap, a thump, a slap, her hand scattering the strands like a wild rake through grass, until, late at night, she would miss completely, and then I knew she was almost asleep. Quietly I would stand my father's picture up and smooth my hair, using the glass as a mirror.

In the distance, somewhere in the depths of the house, a fan belt would kick in and squeak arrhythmically, and dry air would wheeze from floor vents. When my mother's breathing came in time with the fan's gasps I went to my own bedroom, though once I moved my father's picture to his bed table so my mother wouldn't knock it over again. On the day my stepfather and I slept together it was the clanking of the window air conditioner that signaled the presence of the house. At the noise, my stepfather eased out from me and dressed. As he left he turned to me and said, "I know I can trust you to keep this a secret." Then he pulled the door softly closed behind him, like a lover or a thief. I was thirteen then.

My mother brought him home from a bar one night; what I thought I'd heard was confirmed when, in the morning, I went to awaken her for a telephone call. I opened her door quietly and saw her curled on the bed without clothes or sheets, her head at a lopsided angle on the naked sternum of a man I'd never seen, a man with a handsome body and a face that, in repose, looked sad. A breeze blew through the half-open slats of the Venetian blinds and moved her hair. I looked at her face: it was red and puffy, but underneath that, content. She lay on my father's side of the bed, and that picture, an image of a very young man rugged in fishing gear, no more than twenty, and smiling victoriously at his catch, shone over her shoulder. The stranger slept soundly, his hand interposed—but only slightly—between my mother's shoulder and my father's smile, and his penis lay harmlessly like a small white fish a few inches from my mother's mouth. I let them both sleep, unable to break the fragile harmony of the scene: the odor of sex, new to me, mingling with spring; my father and the man lying side by side with my mother; her own, obvious security in their combined presence.

Back in the living room I hung up the phone without taking a message. I turned on the TV and stared through it. My stomach seemed filled with liquid, and as I sat there it boiled out of my guts and into my veins, and my skin turned red with the angry heat of its passage. I felt betrayed, and suddenly my father's picture on the bedside table flashed in my mind. But my mother's stranger was, almost immediately, kind to me. He came in the living room around noon and acknowledged to me what he'd done with a silent shrug of his shoulders. It was a mature shrug, the kind one adult gives to another, and, as a child, I was flattered. The shrug wrecked my resolve, which had risen with the heat of the day: I'd wanted to assault my mother—and him—with my knowledge of their hideous infidelity to my father's memory, but my anger, sourceless from the beginning, retreated into the blazing pit from which it had sprung. His shrug simply said, It happened. There was an apology there if I wanted it, but it was superfluous. Then my glare softened, became a stare, and I found my eyes wandering his body, which was covered now by a loose pair of jeans. "I'm Martin," he said then. I opened my mouth to tell him my name, but the word flew from my tongue before I could voice it. I said, "Did my mother tell you who I was?" He said, "Yes." "Good," I said, for if she'd told him my name, then she must have told him she had a child in the first place. And if there was a child, he must have realized, there would be a father as well, and I believed that my mother had explained what had happened to him. So this man, Martin, knew everything, yet still he'd come. I don't know why I thought this, nor why I took comfort in it, but secure in that knowledge—unaware that none of it was true—I turned back to the television. Martin went in the kitchen.

Later he slipped back in the bedroom with the breakfast I'd heard him making. He took time to stop and tell me there were eggs and bacon on the stove, and plenty of coffee. "Thank you," I made sure I said, pleased he'd considered me mature enough to drink coffee. I ate all the food he'd cooked, though I'd already had both breakfast and lunch, and I drank two cups of coffee, though it raised the gall in my throat. When I finished eating I put on the long apron that hung in the cupboard and started washing dishes. The dishwashing apron, my father had called it, because it was waterproof, and from a long time before I remembered laughing at him encased in its yellow ruffles. After a few minutes Martin entered the kitchen behind me and tousled my hair. His fingers were still greasy from the bacon and I could feel his fingerprints on my scalp after he took his hand away. "Thanks," he said. He grabbed a towel and dried the dishes that I washed and handed to him. I started to explain where everything went, sensing he would need to know this for the future, but he interrupted me. "I know," he said. "I found it all before I cooked." "Right," I said, and turned back to the sink. Martin worked beside me and behind me, and I took as long as I could with the dishes but said nothing more to him, thinking anything that could come out of my mouth would sound childish. When I finished I helped him put away the last of the dishes, and then we pulled a fresh towel from the drawer and dried our hands simultaneously, our skin touching together sometimes within the towel's folds. Then he put his hands on my shoulders and pulled the long apron over my head. "These look ridiculous," he said. "I splash." "Don't be afraid to get wet," he said, then tossed the apron on a counter and went back to my mother's room. The apron had looked old and silly in his hands, and quickly, before I could change my mind, I threw it in the trash. In this way, Martin fitted himself into our lives; sitting on the lid of the trash can, I found it easy to imagine that he'd climbed in my mother's bed while she slept, and for a brief second I felt he could just as easily slip into mine.

My mother had met Martin at a bar; within a month he and I joined together and tried to keep her from returning. We sat on either side of her bed and held a hand apiece, one of hers in two of ours. Martin had moved across the bed since that first day; looking over my mother, I could see my father smiling by his right arm. My mother moaned aloud often, sometimes curses, sometimes pleas for just one drink, sometimes my father's name; Martin and I looked at each other silently over her sweating body. "Oh, goddammit," my mother shrieked, eyes closed, face to the ceiling. "Damn it all to hell." Sometimes I wondered to whom she directed her words, but she never said. And sometimes I wondered what, or whom, she was talking about, but that too was never made clear. "Son of a bitch. Fucking bastard. Stupid little prick." I tried to stare at Martin's eyes and ignore what she said. His eyes showed only sorrow, but I felt it was for both me and my mother. And I noticed also self-pity, but the sum of all that sadness didn't seem to have a dampening effect on him. It was almost as if he were happy to be sad. "Henry," my mother yelled, pulling my eyes back to her. "Henry, why did you do this to me?" Her face was sticky with sweat, and her tongue poked from her mouth after she finished speaking.

I looked back at Martin. He held my mother's hand and sat poised in the chair, as if on view, and his glance at me was long and almost dramatic in its empathy. He stared directly in my eyes; I couldn't break the contact, and felt the struggle register itself on my face as my jaw muscles tightened and my cheek twitched. Martin's eyes and face were steady and relaxed. My mind wavered: dreams rolled in like black clouds. Like death. I felt it coming for my mother and, perhaps, for me. In my chair, I started crying weakly, silently, expecting at any moment for my mother to heave into convulsions as my father had done that day when we'd had to bring him to the hospital for the last time.

When my mother finally ceased struggling that night I left her room to go to my own, leaving Martin caressing her sleeping body. I sat on the edge of my bed and choked my pillow, angry now, no longer crying, and remembered the convulsive way she had gripped Martin's manly hand, and the limp hand she let sit in my girlish one. I wanted to believe, as I held my pillow to my chest, that it was I who held my mother from her rum-and-Cokes, but I knew that she had at some point given that task to Martin. I'd been in my room for only a few minutes when he came in without knocking and sat down next to me on the bed. He did the thing with his fingers in my hair, and when I didn't respond he pried the pillow from my arms and tossed it to the head of the bed. "Pillows are for sleeping," he said. I threw myself backward and at an angle from him on the bed. My head landed on the pillow but my feet still rested on the floor. I lifted my legs up and over Martin, but halfway through the action, my legs raised and spread right in front of Martin's face, I froze, realizing suddenly that I wore only a skimpy pair of underwear. I couldn't decide whether to put my legs back on the floor or complete the movement: indecisive, my legs stuck up in the air like those of a pregnant woman locked in stirrups, and I felt a hot blush across my cheeks. Martin pushed my legs down on the bed with one hand, then lifted the sheet up and covered me to my waist. "I'm sorry you have to see her like this," he said, as though nothing had happened. "But we'll get her through it, don't worry." It was a platitude, I knew, but it wasn't condescension, and I felt his sympathy from his tone, not his words. And I don't remember the words I used—probably these very ones, since I was an unsubtle child—but I told him how afraid I was of losing her as I'd lost my father. I sat up, put my head on his shoulder, and again I cried, gradually slipping down, curling my legs up and around, until I was like a baby half in his lap. Dimly I realized I cried for myself, not my mother, but I made no effort to clarify this realization, only letting my tears, as they always had, cloud my vision. Martin soothed me with soft, breathy exhalations, saying, "I know, I know," in such a way that I believed he did know, had always known, just how I felt, and at the last he loosed a sob and I felt the clear delineation of a teardrop falling on my back and soaking through my T-shirt to my skin. My own crying ceased immediately, with a shudder, as I contemplated that soft wet spot on my shoulder. I lay back, exhausted; he gave my head one more pat good night. The tears in his eyes glistened like golden oil from the glow of the parking lot light outside the window. That night, like all the nights before, he said, "I'm going to sleep with Bea now, to make sure she's okay." But that night his voice was heavy—weighed down, I felt, by the tears I'd caused. Martin bent down and kissed me on the cheek before he left; his lingering lips were dry and soft, and I could feel their imprint on my skin. When he stood up the bed creaked, covering the sound of my suddenly twitching legs rustling the sheets. I swallowed my last sobs with an acrid amount of mucus until the door closed and he was gone, and then I resolved never again to bring pain to a man who would cry for me.

We nursed my mother through a month of withdrawal, and soon drew our strength from her own adamant refusal to drink again, though sometimes her body called for it in shudders so loud the bed shook with her moans of pain. My mother, I remembered, and told Martin to add truth to the memory, had not really drunk until my father became sick. As he worsened, so had she. Her goal seemed clear: to drink herself into the grave and follow him. But after her sadness had passed there was only the alcohol, which seemed determined to kill her though she no longer wanted to die. She always drank alone in her bedroom, sucking down the dank liquid until she was so intoxicated she stumbled out of the house and sang sad songs up and down the gravel streets of our trailer park. Going to the bar had clearly, in my mind, been a move to meet someone like Martin, someone to peel the carcass of drink off her, since she was unable to do it alone. It seemed to me, the more I thought of it, the perfect transformation: my father had brought the bottle into her life with his death; therefore, it would take a new life, a new love, to save her from dying. I was young and I had loved my father as much as my mother, and with a respect that came from seeing her bathe his twisted, convulsing, deteriorated body unaided, even as he tried to force his face under the water. I accepted her solution, and loved Martin as my own.

After a month she got out of bed. She arose at her regular time in the morning as if she'd never been unwell, and had breakfast for Martin and me when we emerged from our sleep. We ate like prisoners enjoying their first free meal after a long confinement. During breakfast she got up suddenly and went to the cabinet where she kept the liquor. There was half a bottle of rum there which we'd stupidly forgotten to throw out. She grabbed the bottle, but went with it to the sink, not the table, and poured it down the drain. Then, overruling our protests, she went to work that same day, saying she'd been gone a month and they wouldn't hold her job much longer, and besides, it was Friday and she'd have the weekend to recuperate if she needed it. I, she said, could take the day off.

Martin and I did the dishes together. We were both very happy, I'm sure, but disoriented, and Martin murmured bemusedly, in a voice with a sound like the flipping pages of a book, something about "only when you're dead." I didn't understand him until years later, after I'd finally made love to a man again without seeing Martin's face at the door and hearing him say, "Keep this a secret." We wandered about the house and idly cleaned, vacuuming, dusting, doing the breakfast dishes. At some point Martin asked me, "Where do you keep the tools?" I led him to the closet and showed him the metal tool box that had belonged to my father. Martin lifted it; I knew from experience that it was too heavy for me, and watched in admiration as the muscles of his arm bulged when he picked the metal bin off the floor. I followed him to the front door and then realized what was up. The lock had broken on the door around the time of my father's death, and it had never seemed necessary to repair it. Now we went at it, but halfheartedly, as though we were tired, and it took us a couple of hours to complete the job. When at last we finished, Martin closed the door, and locked it.

We ate lunch, left the dishes in the sink. The day dragged by. Sometime in the afternoon I slumped on the couch. The energy and tension flowed out of my body like a current, replaced by relief. I suppose I was at last realizing that my mother wasn't going to die like my father, and that Martin wouldn't vanish now that his task was done. But then I only felt joy, an overpowering coolness like an ice-laden cloth on my forehead. I started to cry. Martin came up to me then. He sat down on the couch and folded his hands in his lap like a nervous woman. He didn't say anything to me, didn't ask me why I was crying or why I sprawled on the cushions like a rag doll. Instead, he started crying too. Again, I was amazed by this man who could, unlike all the other men I'd ever known, even my father, cry. I said, I don't know why, "You must love her a lot already." Looking out the window, he said, "I do." Turning to me, he said, "And you too." He paused for a moment as if awaiting a response, and then he said, "It's been hard for both of you." While the sun shone outside, and the wind blew, and cars chewed up the gravel in the parking lot, and a radio that Martin must have turned on without my knowledge played somewhere in the house, we cried, a few feet apart on the couch, not looking at each other. Then my tears stopped on my cheeks, and I sniffled with uneven breaths. Martin's tears ceased as suddenly as they had come, and for just a second I doubted the emotion that lay behind them. But then he reached out and rubbed my hair. His hand rested on my head for a second and I sat like a statue. Then his hand drifted down my face and wiped at a tear. He said, softly, "Come on. Let's stop this." I felt the rough, knuckly hand of a plumber, a hand like my father's. I held it there, and then used his fingers to scratch a soft itch inside the skin of my cheek. And then, slowly, expecting at any moment for him to pull his hand from mine, I put it in my mouth. His fingers tasted like mayonnaise.

A final tear rolled down his cheek. He pulled free from my mouth and took my face in both his hands, one dry, the other wet, and kissed me on the lips. As I closed my eyes I was left with the image of his face being washed by the tear into happiness. There was nothing more then from either of us as we walked to the bedroom: no tears, no touches, no words, significant looks, or communication: no symbols. I wished for a second that he would carry me. Not like a bride, but like a baby, because that is the only way I could imagine myself in my mother's bed. We had sex with enforced quietness. Several times I caught him, and also myself, looking at the bedroom door, listening through the windows, as if expecting some third party to come along and complete our triangle, or dismember it completely. When we finished, I lay in bed for a few minutes after he left. Still looking at the ceiling, I suddenly felt the weight of my father's eyes on me. Then I heard the latch pop open as Martin unlocked the newly fixed door.

That evening, my mother's roast beef gleamed like a small mountain rising from a valley of potatoes, carrots, and onions which swam in a lake of brown juices. Steam bathing her face, my mother said carefully, each word its own proud sentence, "Dinner. Is. Served." "It smells wonderful," Martin said, inhaling audibly. "I know it's a bit much, especially with the weather and all, but it's been so long since I've felt like cooking anything worth eating, that, well, you know." I couldn't see if my mother was blushing or merely flushed as she placed the roast on the table. She sat down between Martin and me. "I think I understand," Martin said, reaching for the loaf of homemade bread and cutting three thick slices. "This meal belongs in a palace," he said, and distributed the bread. The steam out of her face, my mother's skin remained pink. "Oh, you're just saying that." She took his plate and put several pieces of meat on it, then ladled out vegetables and the drippings. She put it back in front of him, then took her plate and did the same. Then she served me. She talked throughout the meal about her first day back at work, about how good it felt to walk home and pass by the bar without feeling the need to go inside, about having someone at home to greet her when she came in. I sat in my corner and watched her and Martin, picking slowly at my food, and every once in a while I said something to pretend I was part of the conversation. But her eyes were fastened on Martin, and his on her, and if she barely touched her plate, it was because she was too busy talking to eat. Martin, though, ate steadily throughout dinner, and the only time he spoke, other than to say I know or I understand, was to compliment her on the food. The meal seemed to be over when Martin pushed away his plate with its half-eaten third piece of apple pie and proclaimed, "I'm stuffed." I got up then to do the dishes, and after a minute Martin started to help me. My mother sat in her chair behind us. She said, "It makes me happy to see you two getting along so well." My hands submerged in a sink of soapy water, my back to her, I didn't say anything. Martin dropped a hand on my shoulder, then ran it through my hair. "You've got a good one here," he said. My mother said she was going to watch some television, then turn in early. "When you're finished," she said, "come stay with me." "Sure," I said, without turning around. "Not you, silly, Martin." "Sure, Bea," Martin said. "I'll be there in about half an hour." "I'll be waiting," my mother said. "Good night, dear." I washed the dishes without looking to see if they came clean and handed them to Martin silently. I felt my mother's hand on my shoulder. Her voice came in my ear. "I said, Good night, dear." I jumped at her touch. "Oh," I said. "Good night." "See you in the morning," she said, and pecked me on the cheek. She'd never done that before, and it seemed hollow to me, like half a kiss. "I'll see you in a couple of minutes," she said. At the same time, Martin and I both said, "See you."

Later, months later, he and my mother were married, and she had me put away my father's condoling picture forever. Martin and I never had sex again; and once, after tousling my hair, he sat up quickly and said he couldn't do that any longer either, and he left my bedroom. Still wanting him, I would look at him for long periods at a time, staring at him through his newspaper until he would drop it tensely and look back at me, softly, sharply, fearfully, always with love and sadness, and once or twice with lust also, but each time he only shrugged it, all of it, away.

The marriage didn't last because my mother only loved him for helping her to overcome drinking and my father's specter. I never saw her fight with him; she only drifted further and further away, and grew more silent until one day all she could say was "I'm sorry—" and he moved out without protest. Later I learned that they'd said things when I wasn't there, had fought and made up often, fucked, talked about me, done the dishes and things like that, lived a separate life while I was out; but then I only hated my mother for sending Martin away even though I loved him more than she. I yelled at her that I would never forgive her if she didn't bring him back, nor would I accept anyone else, for that is what I believed she'd do: go find someone else. With the cruelty of adolescence I screamed, "You're just a slut!" For a moment I stared at the air, as if I could see the word I'd just hurled at my mother. Then she slapped me hard, twice, and said, "Only when I'm dead and gone can you say things like that about me. But while I'm alive you make damn good and sure you mind your place!" On her final words, her voice rose to a scream. I jumped up and down, my arms flying out and hitting the walls so hard that a picture frame filled with family shots fell to the floor—my father, my mother, me; and, still tucked in the frame in front of the glass, new configurations featuring Martin and the two of us. "I loved him!" I yelled, pointing at the broken glass and scattered pictures. "I loved him! And he loved me!" "Shut up!" my mother shrieked. She grabbed me by the hair and threw me down. I lay there and looked up at her. Her face was twisted with rage and disgust. "Don't you ever say that again." I stared at her, my mouth open, tasting blood though I wasn't bleeding. "Get away from me, you foul boy," she said, and turned away. If sleeping with Martin had taught me anything, it had taught me about desire, and I yelled at her retreating form, "You're just pissed because he got what you wanted." She turned, and I saw the shocked expression on her face, and then, before she could hit me again, I ran away.

I was too angry to admit my grief or guilt, and choked on the apology I knew she deserved. Weeks went by and we didn't speak, and I heard it through a friend that Martin had moved from town. Only when my mother dragged out my father's picture did I realize how deeply I'd cut. But the alcohol was gone and the only addiction was to a dead man's memory, and I no more had the cure to that than she could stifle my own sobs for Martin, so I used my pillow to do it to save her any more pain; she clinging to her picture, I to my pillow, we both searched for the essences of men long gone.

I received a letter from him today, you see, that's why I'm remembering all this. It's months old, and has followed me through four different addresses, as if the message it contains is vital. And perhaps it is, though the phrases he used have a curious discordance about them, and the message, if any, has to be picked out carefully: there is a desperate finality in this letter, yet at the same time it is mired in ambiguity. "Dear John," he wrote. "Do you remember our time together?" Sometimes I don't know what I remember, what's real and what's been transformed with time. "I've never forgotten you or your mother, but I had to leave for my sake, and yours and your mother's." All he ever wanted was both of us, and of course he could have neither in the end. That's like Martin, like his tears, his touches, his other empty words. You can have your dreams, he'd said in the kitchen, of how life should be and what your ideal lover should look like and how your first time should go, but he knew—and I do too, now—that you'll never get it, or never be able to hold on to it if you do. Not in this life, he'd told me: only when you're dead.

S O M E O N E   W A S   H E R E

I

Sunday morning's light sneaks in through a six-inch space between the curtains' bottom and the windowsill. It finds me, a fugitive in my bed, awake and awaiting my father's awakening so I can start my day. It's early, he's sleeping, snores penetrate the wall. They come from the living room; though I haven't been up, I know what he looks like, stretched out on the couch: he wears the clothes he worked in yesterday, stained T-shirt and jeans, and his feet, still booted, are propped on the couch's arm. His mouth is open, the skin of his jaw is slack and pale with gray stubble. His clothes smell of cigarettes, his breath stinks of beer.

Last night clings to me as well: cigarette smoke lingers in my clothes, and sand from the river is stuck between my toes. The skin over my stomach is tight with my dried semen, and the taste of someone else's is in my mouth. If I weren't afraid I'd wake my father, I'd eat something to get rid of it. It doesn't taste bad or anything—it's more like an itch, the light, feath-

ery kind that makes you think someone's touching you, but when you look up, there's no one there.

His name was Harry. He had money in oil, he said, and when we finished he gave me a fifty-dollar bill. It was the first time someone paid me, and when he pressed it in my hand, almost coyly, with a nod and a wink, I thought of it as money he'd earned. But during the night I realized I'd earned it, and as I lie here now and try to decide what that means, a second line of light, coming through the vertical slit between the curtains, illuminates the wadded bill on my dresser and turns it almost white.

I wait in bed until past noon, when my father turns on the TV, and then I cook us bacon and eggs, and eat with him in the living room. I thought food would do the trick, but Harry's presence remains, as if he'd ejaculated seconds ago. My tongue wanders my mouth now, searching vainly for something trapped in my teeth and emitting all this flavor, a pepper seed or a clove or something, a cum clove. When my father speaks—he only said my name, he only said "John," but that's how it started—the word slams into my ears and pushes a response out of my mouth before I have time to think. "What?" I say. The sound of my voice startles me; it is clearly, undeniably, pissed off. I look at my father then, I've messed up and I know it, and fear begins to mix with Harry in my mouth.

My father's nostrils flare. "Excuse me," he says, "I didn't mean to disturb you." My swallow isn't quite a gulp. "My tone was directed at my imagination," I say quickly, "not you." My apology is too complicated for my father's hangover, and his eyes narrow. "I sent you to prep school for this—so you can get mad at your 'imagination'?" He puts quotes around the word, like imagination is something I have, he doesn't. I stumble on that. For a moment I think I see what separates us; for a moment I want to embrace him. But what comes out of my mouth is "You sent me to school to make me smart, so don't be surprised if I know a few things." My father's face relaxes into simple anger. "Yeah, I understand that," he says, then stands and walks—to me? the kitchen? Me. He's taken off his clothes since he got up, he wears only underwear now, and he stands so close to me that his torso is all I see. His body seems generic. Wispy chest hairs, a growing paunch: they could belong to any middle-aged man. "So, Mr. Prep School," I hear, and I have to remind myself it's my father talking, "what do you know about this?" He smacks my face. It's the first—no, the second time he's hit me since my mother died.

Spit rushes into my mouth then, and something, adrenaline, I suppose, makes my hands shake. The spit tastes like blood at first, but then I realize, No, it's not blood, it's Harry. I lick my lips to taste him more completely. I blink my eyes, and his torso replaces my father's before me. I stand up. My father's face, heaving as if he'd overexerted himself, threatens to drive away Harry's, so I speak before it can. "I gave a blowjob last night," I say. "Do you understand what that means?"

My father smacks me again. "His dick was small," I say. "I was surprised. I used to think everyone's looked like mine. And yours." My father punches me now, and I do taste blood, and feel it on my chin. "He laughed when he—when he came," I tell my father. "It was strange, but it made me feel so good, the way he laughed, the way, I thought, the way I'd made him *feel* good." Again my father punches me, hard enough to knock me to the chair. I glimpse his fist as it leaves my face. It's smeared with blood, and the blood flashes in the afternoon light. I stand up quickly, determined to keep talking. To fight back. "But the taste," I say, "it really sur-prised me." I lick my lips again, searching for it, but before I find it my father smacks me from both sides, openhanded. He grabs the skin of my cheeks and rattles my head back and forth, and when he's finished he throws me to the floor. My head hits first, I think, I'm disoriented for a minute, it seems like I'm hearing an echo and not actual words. Shut up, I hear, but the words are so faint they lack power.

There's something wrong with my jaw, it's hard to talk. "Herry," I say. "His aye was Herry, allos lie yours." But it doesn't sound like my father's name, not the way I say it, it sounds like my father's voice when he's drunk. "Shut up!" he shouts. I hear him clearly now, and the words, I realize, are filled not with anger but with pain, and I close my eyes then, and my mouth. I've won. My father kicks me in the stomach, and vomit fills my mouth, erasing even the memory of Harry's taste. My father kicks my head. I try to open my eyes then—for some reason I want to see him one last time—but I can't. I wish, suddenly, I wish I'd looked at him while I talked to him, instead of at someone who isn't here. It takes me a long time to think this, and when I have, I open my eyes, and my body isn't in the same place it had been, it's ten feet away, and it's dark, and my father is gone. All I know is that I have to leave here, for good. The only thing I take with me is the money Harry gave me, and the knowledge of how I earned it, and what it cost.

Only later did I realize that I left before answering my father's question. He asked me what I knew about "this"—the smack of his hand. I could have answered him. I could have said, "Not as much as my mother." And in this case, not knowing is worth so much more than knowing.

I read my body now, not as often as I did then, when each bruise was a new book I couldn't quite understand no matter how many times my hands returned to it. Sometimes I hurt myself now and I press on the spot until my mouth fills with an almost-forgotten taste, my head with almost-forgotten images. Sometimes I press my hands together. My right hand—it mostly recovered, though I still can't close it all the way, can't hold a pencil in it—my right hand, though weaker, is larger than my left. It's as large as I remember my father's *hands to be. If you stick a pin in it, I hardly feel a thing, but sometimes it hurts for no reason at all. And what I want to know is, is this—my hand—is this how I am, or how my father was, or both of us, or is it just some clue, some reminder, that someone was here?*

THE SEARCH FOR

WATER

I

Over the years, my father has erected monuments to his prosperity. There are: a gazebo, built from South American hardwood buried in North Dakota granite; an unattached four-car garage, complete with heating and air conditioning; a new wing on the house that is longer, wider, and a story taller than the original building; and, most recently, a Lincoln Continental, which I don't see as my taxi drops me off in our hedge-lined gravel driveway. I try to pay the driver, but she waves me away, saying she's already got her money. Bea, my stepmother, kisses me at the door, dressed for gardening in old jeans and a halter top that exposes her thin, thin back and arms. A pair of dirty gloves flop over her belt, and her exposed skin is shiny with suntan lotion. She smells of sweat and cocoa butter.

She speaks as if distracted, waving a hand at nothing. "He's been sleeping at her place in town. Did you notice the well?" She steps past me on the porch and points across the yard. Near our forest's edge squats a small brick cube topped by a wooden-shingled roof. "One hundred and twenty feet," she says, already yards away from me on her way to the garden. "It's amazing how deep you have to go to find water in Kansas." She stops at the well, leans in, and her back muscles ripple as her arm works an invisible crank. I expect to see a bucket of water with a pewter dipper appear from the shadows, but instead plastic sprinkler heads pop from the ground and begin rotating slowly, their measured streams just overlapping at the edges. "His newest toy," she calls over the sound of squirting jets, and then she watches the lawn until it begins to glow in the sun and water. "It's yours if you want it, John." "The well?" I call, confused. "The house," she answers, and goes in the garden. She closes the gate of the rabbitproof fence behind her. Each of the sprinklers contains its own circular rainbow; they look like multicolored flowers, and I stare at Bea's back through the mirage as she works in the half-grown patch of corn. Then the water stops, the rainbows disappear, and the sprinkler heads retreat into dampened earth. Across the lawn, I hear machinery humming as the well mines for more water.

"I did it all for love," Barclay crooned Friday—yesterday— as he flounced across the small cluttered ruin of his apartment. "I lived for love and I shall die from love." He smiled and rushed to a cracked mirror, checking his makeup to see if any red splotches were visible on his smooth cheeks or the brown dome of his bald head. He learned how to apply foundation in the early sixties, "when a flawless skin meant everything." I've never known his age; he's at least as old as my parents, I think, but somewhere along the line the effects of illness overtook the effects of aging. On the day he dies, he's said, he will awaken early to do his face, and then lie back and smile, and let us find him like that. "It will probably be you, dear John, won't it? Coming in here in your nice white shirts and loose black jeans. No more spaghetti-string tank tops and shredded cutoffs for you. Ah, how I miss the old days!" He giggled like a child at himself, then poked a finger in the brown bags on the table. "And now you bring me all these yucko healthy groceries. What do we have to-day?" he said, his thrice-weekly soliloquy concluded. "The usual," I said, and pulled out organic vegetables and whole-grain pasta and rice, vitamin supplements, soy milk, and unprocessed bread. "Yucko, yucko, yucko," Barclay moaned. "Macro-bioto yucko," and he grabbed a handful of radishes and tossed them in the air with his limp wrists. They fell to the floor like cherry bombs attached to tattered green parachutes. As I picked them up, Barclay rushed by me, his stick-thin legs poking from his embroidered paisley dressing gown. His feet stepped silently in vinyl imitation-gentleman's slippers, and he indiscriminately crushed a radish with one of them. He slumped against a counter. "Oh, my delicate arches," he said, pulling off a slipper and rubbing an already-swelling bump on his left foot. "It used to be I could dance all night in high-heeled glass slippers—Cinderella meets the

Rockettes, you know—and still be fresh enough to escort a gentleman home for some first-class Humpty-Dumpty before bedtime. But now"—he paused dramatically and faked a swoon—"I am undone by a tuber." He rubbed his foot with one hand, then laughed. "Ooh," he said. "Ow. I tickle myself. Ow!" "Radishes help digestion," I said, leaning over to retrieve the pulpy red ball. Piles of rat droppings littered the floor. "Honey," Barclay said, placing a lifeless hand on my shoulder. "I am *beyond* digestion." He laughed hysterically for a second, then swish-limped to the other counter. He pulled several packages from a cabinet and threw them on the table. "The next time you go shopping," he said, pointing, "just bring me these." The table held plastic packages of dehydrated foods—soups and refined pastas mostly. He held one up at an odd angle next to his Cheshire smile. A line of spittle dribbled from his lips. Addressing an imaginary television audience, he said, "Just add water and serve."

Henry grunts in that way he has when I call, and then hollers "Martin!" without covering the telephone mouthpiece, so I receive the full brunt of his shout in my ear. "It's your boyfriend!" Waiting for Martin to pick up, I smell garlic on my fingers from last night's dinner. Sometime between the manicotti and the cannoli Martin had pressed a key to his apartment in my hand; I clutched it so tightly on the train home to Brooklyn that its freshly cut edge bit into my palm, and I sucked a drop of blood to keep it from dripping on my clothes.

When Martin comes to the phone, I hear him arguing with Henry in fierce whispers. "He's not my boyfriend." "What is he then? He's not your lover." "I don't know," Martin says. "Give me the phone." His faint greeting is obscured by the sound of Henry's retreating laughter. "So, what're you thinking?" Martin asks, his voice full of sudden glee. "About what?" "Oh, about anything." His voice lilts, and I imagine his eyes twinkling as they do when he thinks we share a confidence. "I don't know," I say. "I haven't thought about it." "About moving in," Martin says quickly, but his voice is less exuberant. "I don't know," I say again. "What does Henry think about it?" Martin mistakes my question for jealousy. "Don't worry about Henry. He'd have been gone long ago, if—" He cuts himself off. "Anyway, he'll be gone before you move in." Then he talks about the weather in the city, and his job, and about any other thing that seems to enter his head, as if I've been gone for months and not just a few hours. "There was this huge fire in a building down the street. What with the drought and all, they practically tapped the city dry putting it out. Whole building was gutted, and about two dozen families stranded." "I know," I say, cutting him off. "I read about it in the paper." Then I tell him my stepmother needs my help in the garden. "When will I hear from you?" he asks, and I gather from his plaintive tone that he means, When will I hear that you're moving in with me? "My parents have offered me the house out here," I say quickly, before he can ask another question. "But I don't know what's going to happen yet."

My old bedroom takes the contents of my new suitcases grudgingly. Drawers which years ago held only my underwear and T-shirts and jeans now overflow with gardening magazines, sewing supplies, all types of yarns and knitting needles, half-woven macramé projects, jigsaw puzzles, books of completed crosswords, and down in the bottom drawers, my old underwear and T-shirts and jeans. I take these clothes out now and throw them away, then replace them with adult clothing: underwear that has changed from white jockey shorts to baggy boxers and one worn bikini that I don't remember packing and also throw away; plain T-shirts give way to new ones with slogans like "B is for Boy" and "AIDSwalk '87"; and only the Levi's look the same, though these new ones are larger than those I discard.

In the garden my stepmother sweats furiously, the drops rolling off her nose and spotting the dry earth. She wears her gloves now, and they are caked with flaky soil; a few streaks of dirt fill the creases of her forehead from where she has wiped her brow. She digs in the ground with her fingers to pull out large marigold bushes by their roots, tugging sometimes three or four times when the plants resist. I sit down on a small mound and draw my knees close to my chest. I pull a long blade of grass and chew on it, but I spit it out when I taste its bitter juice. I know if I wait long enough, my stepmother will tell me what's going on. She does: "That was a cucumber mound you're sitting on," she says, then pushes me down when I start to rise. "Don't worry," she says, "it never sprouted." She digs out another marigold plant and tosses it aside. "I read in one of my gardening magazines that if you plant marigolds in thick rows between your vegetable patches, the flowers will draw the bugs away from what you really want to be growing, which is your food." She talks and works, and seems to be speaking to the plants, as if chastising them. "They offered it as an alternative to pesticides, and I wanted to get away from all that artificial stuff anyway." "It didn't work?" I say, when she seems to have finished. "No, it didn't. I think the marigolds actually lured bugs in the garden, and after they'd finished decimating the flowers, they moved on to my vegetables." She pulls a bloom off one plant and shows it to me; it's half-eaten, and the orange petals are brown-edged where insects have chewed. "Anyway, I thought I'd get these out of my way now. I'm always tripping over them." The garden has been my stepmother's passion for the last three years, and she invests six to eight hours daily on the huge plot. Now, pulling out plants, she seems to be unraveling all that work somehow, loosening the ties that have held the garden together through three harsh summers. When I stand up, I see the flowers lying behind her and stretching out before her. They divide the garden like borders on a patchwork quilt, and now I see why the garden seems to be unraveling: the plants she has already picked make frayed edges, their green leafy parts and bright orange flowers spilling over their lines into the corn, cucumbers, and tomatoes, while those that remain waver a little in the hot breeze, like loose threads waiting to be plucked. I put a hand on Bea's back, slick with perspiration. Her hair, tied in a ponytail, sprays across her skin, matted to it by sweat; a few gray strands stand out distinct from the brown ones. Were this a romance, I think, I could trace the length of each gray strand with a finger; and if this were fantasy, the gray would return to brown under my hand. But I only ask, "Do the flowers really hurt?" Bea sits up at my words and shucks off her gloves. "No," she says tiredly. "They don't hurt." She gets up and walks to the hose, abandoning her gloves on the ground like empty seed shells. "I hurt," she says, dousing herself. The sweat is washed from her body, replaced by water pumped from one hundred and twenty feet beneath the garden.

All I know is that he left her for his secretary, who is young and thin and pretty, and went to high school with me for nearly a year. She blushes as she lets me in her small house, murmuring, No one thought we'd ever see you again: once inside and past her drab yard, I recognize my father's taste and money in the furnishings: overstuffed floral-printed chairs, imitation oil seascapes, and a three-inch-thick shag the color of wet red clay. My father insists we take his car to dinner, not the Volkswagen I'd pulled out of the garage for the first time in years. He'd bought it for me when I was eighteen to entice me to stay home, but the odometer has barely a thousand miles on it, and I'm twenty-six now. My father pulls his car from an innocuous, tin-sided, padlocked carport, and we drive away, leaving his mistress in the doorway.

"I'm not going to make any excuses," he says over a red plate of spaghetti and meatballs. "The life went out of our marriage." He leans over with the napkin tucked in his collar; pushed forward by his girth, it drifts across his plate. He whispers, "She stopped getting her period, you know, and after that, she just dried up." He sits back and examines me to see if I've understood. "Well, I'll tell you something. I'm still not ready to be old, even if she is." The first time he wasn't "ready to be old" came nineteen years ago, when he married Bea three years after my mother died. He twirls a forkful of pasta on his spoon and stuffs it in his mouth as if to stop himself from saying anything more, because, after that, he remains silent for the rest of the meal. We listen to the tinkling of silver and crystal, to the low voices from other tables and occasional shouts from the kitchen. Piped-in Italian music plays on a revolving loop, and the second time "That's Amore" comes on, our meal finished, my father sits back and listens to the song. As the last strains die out, he says, cautiously, "So how are you doing in that department?" "What do you mean?" I say. He pauses, and cleans his hands before speaking. "Are you sleeping with anyone?" he asks, and quickly wipes his mouth and looks at the other tables. Leave it to my father to boil it down to the big boff-o-rama. Barclay would say that, not me. "No," I tell him. "I'm sleeping with no one." "But—" my father says, because I haven't clarified the matter in exactly the way he wishes. "But there is someone who wants to sleep with me. I'm just not sure I want to sleep with him." My father sighs at this last word, then quickly regains his composure. He runs a hand through his thinning hair, and as often happens, some of it gets caught in the gold band of his Rolex. He winces as he snaps the errant strands from his scalp. "So," he says, "you're not still doing what you used to?" "I make house calls now." The skin of his cheeks and forehead covers his eyes in a squint. "House calls?" he asks. "I work for a hospice." His face brightens. "Oh, that's good." "No," I say, "it's not, really. But it's necessary, and it's safe." "Safe," my father repeats, and then makes a business of signaling the waiter and paying the bill. He gulps a glass of water as we leave the table, and on the way out the door grabs a thick handful of chocolate mints, and he eats them all during the car ride home.

My stepmother wasn't always idle. She had a nursing degree and worked in a small, poor rest home for the first few years of her marriage to my father. She took me with her one summer, because my father's contracting business looked like it wouldn't make it and bringing me to work cost less than a babysitter. My stepmother, always busy at the home with some real or made-up task, left me alone to wander the halls or play in the courtyard, surrounded by old people in baby-blue or pastel-pink bathrobes forever falling open to expose worn pajamas underneath. One woman, Mrs. Derkman, never moved from her bed; she lay there with her legs curled to where her breasts used to be, her arms holding them in place, her hands balled in fists of powerless defiance. No one visited her. She stared at the wall all day, blinking sometimes, but never speaking. Her silent mouth and fixed eyes fascinated me. When I fed her—for after a while my stepmother allowed me to—she ate without looking at me or the spoon. Her mouth opened when she smelled food, and after swallowing it opened again. If I waited too long between bites she closed her mouth and wouldn't open it even if I pressed a spoon filled with vitamin-enriched oatmeal—the only thing she could eat—to her lips. I would leave the room, wait a moment, and re-enter. She had no sense of time, it seemed, and her mouth sprung open the moment she smelled the food again. Is this sickness, I sometimes wondered, or is it age, or is there a difference between the two? When she died the next year, the morticians had to break her joints to straighten her limbs so she would fit in her casket, and they found that her fingernails had grown a half inch into her palms, and her buttocks were two large bedsores. I didn't see this, though; my father refused to allow me near the home after he came one day and saw me laughing with two old men, one of whom shamelessly played with his genitals

through his pajamas. "All that death!" my father bellowed.
"All that degeneracy. I don't want my boy to be a part of it,"
and he worked twice as hard then to make his business succeed so my stepmother could bring me home and raise me
without death or degeneracy ever touching my life.

I remember little of my seven months in high school, save
that, at fourteen, in gym, my sexuality and sexual preference
were both revealed to me by a sudden erection in the showers.
I don't know why but I panicked, and ran away across the
slick tiled floor. The other boys' laughter followed me; they
were the last people ever to do that. Brown bricks make the
building: brown bricks and straight walls and square corners,
and it seems that the plain mess just fell here, that human
hands couldn't possibly have constructed such a lifeless husk.
Inside, the halls reverberate with the sound of my footsteps,
and an occasional laugh comes from behind the closed door
of a summer school class. A silver-haired woman dressed in
a gray polyester skirt and matching sleeveless sweater, her fat
feet swelling from red high-heeled pumps, hobbles up to me.
She looked the same twelve years ago, though even then I
didn't know her name. "May I help you?" she says, and I
quickly answer, "Just reminiscing." "Just what?" she says,
cupping an ear toward me, though I doubt she's hard-of-
hearing. "Remembering," I say loudly, giving her the benefit
of the doubt. "Strolling down memory lane." I put an arm
around her shoulder and pull out a long-unused smile and

give it to her. She steps along with me, I at her pace. She's confused, I can tell, and flattered, as I point out my home-room, show off the locker where I kissed my first girlfriend, and stop outside the glass-walled cafeteria where another boy and I once got into it. I don't tell her that he chased me here from the gym, nor do I mention that I pushed his face through the plate glass door; I call it a scrap, and laugh, and she says, "Boys will be boys," and laughs with me. There is the exit, I think, through which I once ran in fear. Today I stop in the doorway and wave at an old woman whose name I still don't know. "Come back some time," she says. "Sure," I say: the criminal always returns to the scene of the crime.

My stepmother rarely cooks. She drinks spring water through the morning and afternoon, and then orders out for dinner, usually something that can be delivered and eaten from its own disposable container: Chinese food, Italian food, things like that. Sunday comes and goes, then Monday and Tues-day, Wednesday and Thursday, Friday and another Saturday. How my parents divide their possessions I don't know. My stepmother comes in after meeting with him at his office in town. "Well," she says, "he'll keep the business, but I'll get forty percent of anything it makes and fifty percent if he ever sells it." That's only fair, considering her inheritance financed its start. "He'll keep the Lincoln, of course, and I'll keep the Jeep." The sticky point seems to be the house. "If we sell it, we'll split it sixty/forty, my way." She looks at me. "But that's only if we sell it. We'd like to give it to you, but we both think you should live here if we do. We don't want it to fall to ruins, and there's no sense paying to keep it up if no one's here. Do you want it?" she asks bluntly. I look at the family pictures mounted on the walls of the new living room, hoping that in one of them I'll find a reason to accept the house or decline it. But the images are hidden behind glass frames which reflect the lamplight like puddles catching the morning sun. "I don't think you should sell it," I say. "Why don't one of you keep it?" My stepmother sighs. "John, that's a moot point by now. Your father and I have been over and over this. We both put a lot into this place, and it wouldn't be fair if one of us got it at the expense of the other. The only fair thing to do is give it to you or sell it."

She lets me think about it for a while, and one week consumes another, and then another. Summer clamps down like a vise, wringing us dry, and the leaves on the catalpas flap like dry laundry on the line. The sprinkler system cuts off even faster now, and it can be used only during the evenings, since the combination of water and sunlight during the afternoons only magnifies the heat, singeing the grass. My stepmother works in the garden less and less each day. We sit around the house for hours; Bea listens to Vivaldi and Bartók, humming absently under her breath and starting new needlepoint or knitting projects that she'll shove in a drawer as soon as the hot spell breaks. Her cigarette smoke drives me from the living room, first to my bedroom, but that room swelters in the old, un-air-conditioned part of the house, so I retreat to the basement. There, I sift through boxes labeled John's Things, boxes filled with toys that grow progressively larger and more masculine. Lincoln Logs give way to a stainless steel Erector set; a rusted tricycle finds its replacements in a BMX motocross bike and a racing ten-speed. There are bats and rackets and hockey sticks and all sorts of balls, and all of them are alike in their dusty age. Two boxes contain only war toys: fake guns and knives and combat fatigues, and a folding shovel still crusty with dirt from its last long-ago use. In the bottom of one box I find a doll my real mother gave to me. My father had shaken the bead-stuffed thing in Bea's face one night and screamed, "This is what destroyed my little boy!" I sneered at him and swatted the doll from his hand, telling him I didn't even remember its name. This was right before he'd given me the car. My father looked at the doll, its long dress folded above desexed legs by the force of its landing. "Pretty Boy," he said. "You called it Pretty Boy when your mother was alive."

Barclay died today. Martin calls and says, "He was done up like a French whore." "What finally did it?" I ask. He'd seemed on a rebound when I left. "Was it the pneumonia?" "No," Martin says, and I can't tell if his voice is leering or saddened over the telephone. "It was the rat poison you bought." He starts to ask me about moving in again, but I cut him off. "Listen to me, Martin, listen to me for just a second." Martin tries to say something, but I cut him off again, keep talking. "Barclay used to bathe me. Do you see what I'm saying, Martin? He used to wash the smell of them off me. He'd fill the tub with water that was almost boiling —he'd spike it with pots of water he'd cooked on the stove to get it that hot. He used to steal the best soaps and shampoos and stuff, for me, he never used them on himself, only on me. He even had a little brush that he used under my fingernails, and when he finished washing me, he had clean clothes for me, and he put them on me and combed my hair and sent me out again. And I always knew I was done for the night when instead of clothes he'd wrap me in this robe he'd got somewhere, probably stole it too, this beautiful silk robe that was too small for me. Fits you like a miniskirt, Barclay'd say, and he'd put this on me just to walk me ten feet from the tub to the bed and take it off me and tuck me in, and then, after I was asleep, he'd get in bed too and wake me up with his kisses, and with him I never had to do anything but I always wanted to no matter how many, what kind I'd done that night. Something Barclay did always had me wanting him. After we were finished he washed me again, this would be my fourth or fifth bath of the night and I'd tell him it was okay, let's just sleep, but he always insisted, he said, Honey, if you don't know it by now, then let me set you straight: this girl ain't no better than the rest of 'em." I stop then, not because that's all there is but because I know I've said too much and because Martin is crying on the other end of the line. My own cheeks are dry. "Martin?" I say. His voice snuffles out, wet and angry, "But he was sick, John, sick, don't you see that?" At first I think he means AIDS, and then, when I realize he doesn't, I hang up. I want to say something, just one thing that will sum it all up—I want to tell Martin he's wrong, and I want to tell him he's right too—but I realize that saying what's right and what's wrong isn't enough in this case. And it's not important either, now. Barclay's dead. There's only one thing, really, that I still want to tell Martin. The rat poison, I'll say some time: I bought it for the rats.

My father takes me to dinner again. We go to the same Italian restaurant and order the same food, and over dinner it seems he re-explains the situation to me using the same words as last time. As we drive back to his girlfriend's house in the climate-controlled shell of his Lincoln, he says, "One thing you have to remember, John, before you judge me, is that I love her. I'll always love her." Who does he mean? I wonder, for there are three candidates here. I'm about to ask, when he stops at a red light. In the car next to us two high school girls with wild hair and tan breasts bursting from their bikinis stare at my father's car, either in admiration or because they are preening, using his tinted windows as a mirror. My father stares at them behind the safety of his one-way glass wall. What would he do, I think, if I suddenly pressed the button that unrolls the window? Even as I make my move, the light turns green and he floors it, blowing the Toyota off the road—again, Barclay's phrase—and the force of his acceleration knocks my hand away from the button, so I never get the chance to expose him. Looking at my hand, I feel relieved that I was prevented from acting rashly. It would only have led to trouble. Beside me, my father raises his eyebrows in a minute, whimsical gesture, and surprises me by murmuring, "Ah, the beauty that does not belong to me."

Out of bed early one morning and I feel like my old self again, though which self that is I don't know. It's rained while I slept and the pale water sluicing down the windowpanes mixes with sunlight to form transparent shadows on the floor. I pull on a pair of shorts and wander outside. My stepmother works in the yard with a pair of garden shears in her ungloved hands. I watch her and see that she's cutting dandelions. They've finally bloomed, thanks to the rain, and thousands of bright gold suns litter the lawn, and they're vaguely beautiful, though Bea has always abhorred them. I set up a lawn chair and watch her attack the dandelions with the shears all morning and afternoon, cutting and cutting, reminding me of the mother of Dinesen's "Sorrow-Acre." By evening, somehow, she has finished the entire lawn, and rakes the wet dandelions in a huge pile. Today was cooler than days past, overcast, but the sun's invisible rays, amplified by the rain-laden clouds, have burned both our skins. Now my stepmother stands at the pile, and its dimensions dwarf hers for the moment; now she douses it with gasoline from a can; now it's alight, spewing dank smoke, and the flames seem to magnify the gold of the dandelion heads before consuming them. I walk over to her with the hose. "Don't you want this, just in case?" "No," she says, holding her stiff-fingered hands away from her body. "Let it burn itself out." She turns to me. "And I don't care if it takes everything with it." The look in her eyes frightens me; they challenge me to a reply which I can't offer. "Besides," she says, thrusting out her hands, "I couldn't hold the hose anyway." In the light from the flames I can see her palms are covered with blisters, most of them ripped open. She turns back to the pyre, face glowing and rapturous, and says, "We're selling the house. Go back to your man. You don't really want to be here." I barely hear her, staring at her hands, which seem to be letting go of something, setting it down and pushing it far away. Water from the hose dribbles to the ground and soaks my feet. I reach for what she's setting down, reach and reach—my hands grip the hose so tightly—but I can't find it. Eventually I abandon the effort, turn the water off. Just as the fire burns out, Bea says, "I didn't get them by the roots, you know. They'll be back next year." She speaks as though we'll still be here, but then I think, The roots she speaks of, they stretch far beyond the borders of this house.

Martin calls me and demands an answer. Here is his story: I've known you for over a year, John, and all you ever let me do is kiss you on the lips with a closed mouth. You cook me overspiced food and I buy you new books which you refuse to read. I tell you what plays are worth seeing, but you take me to the beach instead and don't go in the water. I tell you I love you, and I have to wring a response from you, but you always say you love me too. You won't take anything from me, and you won't give me anything; you beg me not to leave, but you offer me no reason to stay. You call when you wake up sweating in the middle of the night, and I listen to you cry on the phone and wish I could hold you and wipe the dampness from your skin. I buy the magazines and videos that still have you in them, and I use them to get off, and then I burn them. You tell me all about Barclay, and I tell you nothing about Henry, save that he exists. Over a year and your dinners have become incredibly elaborate, hours-long productions and your bookshelves are overflowing and Barclay is dead. You didn't even make his funeral. I made Henry move out. This doesn't mean things have changed, really, just that they could. Change. Just know that I'm not afraid of it, John, whatever it is, okay?

So there's that.

Henry is Martin's lover, but I am the one Martin loves. I sleep with no one but I care for Barclay. Years ago, when I was fourteen and newly run away from home—from school, really, where Eric Johnson's slashed face probably still bled —Barclay dressed me in a child's tuxedo and top hat and presented me at the first of many Harvest Balls, "where the fruit is you." He watched and hummed Judy as I gave it to an aging drag queen named Anisette, "like the drink, darling." Barclay's hot hand clapped me on the shoulder when I'd finished; I sweated but felt dried out. "That was so marvelous, dear, for your first time, but now let me show you how it's really done." He upended me, and Anisette sat on my chest while he did it, sipping a cocktail, her Scarlett O'Hara gown pulled above her hairy waist and choking me with its dusty ruffles. I've been thirsty ever since. Anisette still straddled me when she handed Barclay several crumpled bills from her purse, and I remember growing confused then: behind the dry mountain of her body my inner thighs still twitched with pleasure, but in front of her bulk I sucked in vain for the air and water that poured, without my control, from my mouth and eyes and nose, forced out by Anisette's unbearable weight on my chest. And I must tell you: this is the hollow center of my being, the one thing in my life I don't understand, and from it I've learned not to trust my instincts, not to act, because I know that I have no control over the consequences of those actions. "Oh, baby," Barclay had leaned close and whispered to me: "Don't cry. I love you, I really do. I'll love you till the day I die." And then, laughing, he walked away. And it's not that Barclay could joke about his own death that bothered me, not then, when death was a new thing, nor later, when his ice-cold skeletal hand clutched mine through three bouts of pneumonia and he still laughed when he could summon the breath. It's just that when he placed his hands on my body, squeezing in all the places that used to belong to him, and kissed me with his cracked tongue, it seemed he laughed at mine as well. "No," I told him, "it's not the old days anymore." "Don't act like a little boy," he said. "There never were any old days. There's no difference between then and now."

And perhaps he's right, for when I return to my school the woman still hobbles the hallways in her gray skirt and sweater and garish pumps. She looks at me and smiles quickly; her hands flutter to touch her dyed hair, and she asks me what I'm doing here. "I'd like to take you for coffee," I say, and she glances around to see if anyone else has heard my offer. She protests for a moment—"Well, I don't know, I hardly know you"—but soon says yes. In a small bright café we drink coffee and she tells me her name is Mrs. Enniger. I let her talk for an hour, and then, walking at her snail's pace toward her house, we pass a shoe store. "Shoes," I say. "I want to buy you shoes." "What?" she says as I whisk her inside. I point to her pumps and say, "If you keep wearing those, you'll be on a cane in five years." She says, "No, no, I'm fine," but when I ease her shoes off she sighs audibly; her feet are swollen and misshapen, and it takes several minutes before they appear normal. I slip a pair of rubber-soled, orthopedic shoes on her. "Try these," I say. She stands, takes a few tentative steps. "I feel funny," she says. "I've been walking on stilts for too long. But these are so comfortable!"

She smiles at me, sits down, looks at her feet, says, "But they're old lady's shoes." Look, look, look in the mirror, I want to say: You're not old. Mrs. Derkman was old, Barclay was old. But I only say, "I won't force them on you." "Are they expensive?" she asks. "They cost me nothing." She wears them home. At her house, old habits send me walking in behind her, a hand on her waist slipping lower. I stop before she really notices, but one hand flutters to her hip where mine had been. She jokes, "You've changed my life," and perhaps I have, but mine, I realize, is still the same.

The smell of tempura and soy sauce fills Martin's apartment one evening. Boxes labeled John's Things flood the floor. Toy pistols and pots and pans mix like childhood and adulthood all around me. They are the legacy of both my parents: though my father bought everything, it was my stepmother who saved each item. If it was just this one thing and nothing more—just these boxes—then I would puzzle it through until I understood it. But it's not: it's this and it's everything. Henry found his own place in no time, and I planted a few flowers on Barclay's grave, thinking that my mother's lies untended somewhere in Kansas. When I fed him, I ask myself now, did I really want to keep him alive, or just some memory of my past? My stepmother has moved to the West Coast with a boyfriend and my father has gone alone to Colorado. They'll call me, I imagine, or I'll call them: it's inevitable. Here is Martin, his arms on my body, saying, I love you, make love

to me. Bring me a glass of water, I say; I was going to drink
it but then I dip my fingers in the glass like a young shoot
and trace patterns on Martin's body with my water fingers,
and it's okay, because he hasn't seen the movie where I did
it first, following a script, watched by a camera, burned under
sun-bright lamps, having sex with a man who would be dead
in six months. Behind me now, Martin says he'll take care
of me no matter what, and I say, but not to him, "No."

TRACKS

∎

Because there was nothing left of me, I went with him. The world accumulated history as each second passed, but I sloughed it off as though my body were coated in wax. I wanted to remember nothing, foresee nothing, there was nothing I wanted to know about myself. But him: a scar ringed his left eye, a white circle with red edges, and a drop of blood floated in his blue iris. "My father," he said wearily. "A broken Coke bottle." That was enough for me—almost too much—and I followed him from Port Authority to a taxi without further questions.

I had run away, arrived here only hours before; in a month I'd be sixteen. I'd abandoned my past, poured it from my life like liquid from a bottle. I ignored what I already knew—that a bottle is never as important as what fills it—and I also tried to ignore the details which began to pile up in me like separate ingredients waiting to be mixed together. Outside the car, grime covered everything, blurring edges like a soporific; X's flashed on marquees, announcing something which I knew to be at the center of my situation. Inside, the boy from Port Authority shivered, sweated, crossed his arms over his stomach. "God, I need a fix," he said. Though I didn't know what he meant, I didn't ask. I just said, "Me too." He looked at me then, and I returned his stare. His eyes mocked me, told me I'd messed up, forced me to look down. That's when I saw his hands. Red lumps deformed every knuckle, and at the center of each lump was a tiny brown scab; a few oozed pus. History was revealed there, a process of decay that had happened one bump at a time. Revolted and fascinated, I stared until he lifted his shirt and folded his hands into the concave shell of his stomach. Looking up, I saw he'd turned to the window. His eye was hidden, but I could see part of the scar that ringed it. It didn't seem so horrific compared to his hands. Even under cloth, they made me want to shudder. And then I realized he'd hidden them under his shirt: he was ashamed of these wounds, and I suddenly knew that, unlike his eye, they were self-inflicted. It was something I'd never thought before: that people might hurt themselves on purpose.

The taxi lurched forward like a time machine, momentum claimed my attention. We gathered speed recklessly until the car overflowed with it, and because it's easy for me, I forgot everything except the street, which slapped at us like a swung belt. Then the car slammed into a hole and bucked out of it at an angle, and when the squeal of the tires had left my ears and we were again under control, I found myself clasping the boy's arm. But as soon as I felt him between my fingers, so *thin, so weak, my grip softened, and then I was merely holding him, not holding on to him. A thought seized me: I wanted to protect him. I wanted to protect him because, though it's easy to forget things, it's also hard not to remember. I was remembering my mother: her thinness, her fragility, her weakness, and death. I would have remembered more, but he grabbed me, my hand: my right hand. He pulled it off his arm and held it, flipped it like a pancake. "What's up?" he said, "what's with your hand?" More memories flooded my brain, and they escaped through my mouth: "My father," I said. "The sole of his boot." The only answer I could give, as free of history as possible, it still contained a force that stunned me, propelled by the weight of everything I'd lost, and hinting, somehow, at things I had yet to gain.*

He looked at me for a long time, and then he looked at my hand again, and then he looked at his own hand, which now held mine. It was pretty ruined. His, I mean. He leaned forward then, told the driver to stop. As soon as we had, he pulled me out. "Run," he yelled, already backing away. The driver hopped out of the cab. "Hey, somebody got to pay for the ride," he called, but the boy drowned him out. "Beat it, John!" he yelled. "Make tracks! Get lost!" At this, he took off. The taxi driver came around the car. I could see he wasn't going to help me, that no one would help me. That's when I started running. I tried to follow the boy's directions: I tried to get lost. But though I easily lost my way in that long-ago city, the boy from Port Authority had stirred up something I would never escape: memory and emotion, and thoughts of people I could never possess. History.

I know now that the boy from Port Authority was the first man I ever loved, and the last person I ever trusted. I know now that it's always been that way with me: I will love a man at the slightest sign of weakness, but I will never trust anyone, for trust makes you weak. For years I searched for him, around the Square, in Port Authority, and I always double-glanced at any thin sandy-haired boy I passed on the street, seeking, but never seeing, the scarred left eye. I thought I might see his picture in the paper, in a notice announcing his death. You could tell with him, not just from his hands, not just from his face or from the drop of blood that was melted into the blue of his eye, but from the way he held himself, just as my mother had. With people like that, it's not a question of when they'll die, but a question of how, and how soon. And though his eye haunts my stories—it most resembles a bull's-eye, a target waiting for an arrow—and though I've seen hands on many people destroyed even more than his by track marks, still, what I feel most when I think about him are arms, so thin that the bones seem pliant. The arms encircle a stomach, trying to contain a destructive urge which will not be held back. What that was, for him, is easy to say: heroin. What it is for me—as it was for my mother—is harder to say, not because the answer is any less obvious, but because, after everything that's happened, it makes no sense: love. And trust.

THREE NIGHT

WATCHMEN

■

Upon my couch at night
I sought the one I love—
I sought but found him not.
"I must rise and roam the town,
Through the streets and through
    the squares.
I must seek the one I love."
I sought, but found him not.
I met the watchmen
who patrol the town.
"Have you seen the one I love?"
    —*The Song of Songs* 3:1–3

What language do you speak?

The words come from nowhere, in quiet neutral tones, and for a moment I'm confused. As I enter a small dirty office, the breath of a wheezing air conditioner seeks out the hollow between my damp shirt and sweating back, filling the space with cold vapor. A pair of thin young lovers share each other's laps on a vinyl couch. One of them, or perhaps the pink-dressed woman at the desk, has asked the question. "French," the girl says now, giggling; *"Moi aussi,"* the boy replies, and then the lovers start to speak haltingly in a language from which I'm excluded. They glance in my direction, then return to the boy's application in conspicuous silence. I take one from the fleshy hand of the woman at the desk, and in what seems like seconds, I have a job. As I leave the woman calls, "So, you got no trouble staying up nights?" and her laughter, and the hesitating laughter of the lovers, follows me into the evening heat.

As I walk home from the interview, a car's lights catch me from behind and cast my pale shadow long and wavering in front of me. As it speeds past, the driver leans out to yell, "Jesus, buddy, get out of town." Then he's gone, and I can't help but wonder if it will be like this every time I walk home from the plant. Soon enough I'm back at our curtained dark house. Martin lies on the couch, sleeping. His chest expands and contracts, filling and then deflating his black T-shirt, which seems to become an empty sack each time he exhales. The ridge of his triceps casts a tiny shadow across the tanned skin of his right arm. His black jeans are loose on his body; inside them his legs bend at the knee, and his bare feet are shoved in the crack between the couch's cushions as though they're cold. I'm afraid when I find him like this, afraid I'll roll him over and he'll dissolve like sugar in water, leaving his clothes empty, his body gone except for his feet, which burrow for warmth on a summer evening. He speaks sud-

denly, a half-mumbled greeting, his voice obscured in the
space between his mouth and the back of the couch. To his
back I say, "Did you sleep here all day?" He sits up, yawns,
nods. Small lines crease his left cheek, and his black hair is
matted like a coarse brush. I go to him and touch the red
lines. "Bed face," I say, smiling at him, but the lines smooth
away at my touch, leaving his skin unwrinkled, a little paler.
Realizing he's not at work, I ask, "Why?" He smiles, telling
me he got the night shift at Heller's Warehouse, and asks me
about Carmel. "I got the job," I say. He kisses me, and tells
me almost shyly that we'll be working the same hours now.
I put my hands under his shirt. "I don't care about working,"
I say. "We'll have the same free time." After kissing me again,
he asks me if I'm tired. "A little," I admit. He kisses me a
third time, suggests we go to bed. I pull my hands from under
his shirt. "First tell me about it again. Tell me what it's like."
Just remember, he says, how he always says it: men everywhere. In their own bars, their own cafés, their own clubs.
"Their own apartments?" I ask. Their own apartments, he
says: hundreds of them, just like ours, but bigger sometimes,
or smaller, and right next to everyone else's, windows and
curtains open, pictures on the wall. And the men hug and
kiss and make love with whomever they choose, and when
they go out they display themselves, slicking back their hair
and rolling up their sleeves to show off their arms, or no shirt
at all, and tight jeans that show off everything else. They
hold hands even, or at least link arms, they wear jewelry and

they strut like peacocks, and there are hundreds of them, thousands, everywhere you look.

"And someday soon, we'll live there," I add. Without answering me, Martin gets up to go to the bedroom. Weariness seizes me as we climb into bed, and Martin's face, I see, looks as haggard as I feel. Our hands seem to follow the path of least resistance and soon—without ever needing a condom—we are sticky and Martin is sleeping beside me, and the drone of the window water cooler fills my head as I lie next to him, awake. It sounds like a light rain shower. I stay in bed and listen to it, unable to sleep, and then I start to imagine that it *is* raining, that the green bedspread we lie on is a grassy hillside, and I imagine that the sweat and semen and saliva which soaks our bodies is really clean water. Beside me, Martin moans lightly in his sleep, and his hand reaches out, looking, I suppose, for mine. I watch his fumbling fingers for a moment, and then, almost reluctantly, I take them in my own.

The first night on the job, my uniform feels stiff on my skin, scratchy. The blue polyester seems washed out already; the yellow stripes running down the sides of my legs stand out boldly, but the stitching that holds them in place is weak, and I can see that in a few weeks it will begin to fray. My feet drag in their thick-soled boots, and the hat I wear, with its gilt badge, is almost comic. This late, the only work being done at the plant is automated, and my walk through Carmel's deserted streets is punctuated by the faint whirs and clicks of machines. At the end of the row of buildings I see the guard-house. Barely larger than a phone booth, it's illuminated by a streetlamp from without and overhead fluorescents within. It crowds up against the tall chain-link fence, and inside, a short person in blue jeans leans against a counter, sipping from a styrofoam cup held in both his hands.

"Coffee?" he asks as I push open the door and feel a gush of air-conditioned air. Every room of this plant, it seems, is climate-controlled. "No thanks." "Take it," he tells me. "You'll need it. Nights are long out here." He turns his face to me: I see cloudy blue eyes and fleshy cheeks that descend below his chin in deep runnels. His neck, though, is thin, making his face seem even fatter. "Maybe later," I say, and turn to face the plant. It seems alive now, as if behind all those walls are people moving around again after stopping and hiding while I walked by. Turning back to the man, I say, "I don't have much trouble staying awake." "Sure," he says, "suit yourself. Pot stays on all night." He sets his cup down on loose papers stained with a hundred coffee rings and wipes his hands on the shirt stretching tightly over his stomach. Coming the two steps to me, he sticks out his hand. "I'm Charlie," he says, "Charlie Goertz. "Well, kid, you got me for three days. Best get started now." "Sure," I say, and sigh quietly and quickly. If Charlie notices he doesn't say anything.

*   *   *

"It's not as big as it looks," I tell Martin later the same day. "Nearly two miles around the fence, and on this side I can see our house as we do the walk." Martin got home a half hour before me, but already he'd fallen asleep on the couch and I had to wake him. He'd only taken the time to change from his uniform into a gray T-shirt and brown jeans; the industrial white pants and shirt lie on the floor by the couch, abandoned like shed skin. When I brush Martin's hair from his face the brown strands ripple like wheat. "Actually, I can only see the house on the third walk, since the first two times it's dark out, and of course there aren't any lights on in here. But it's nice, you know, to be able to see this place from there." I pause; beside me, Martin is quiet, maybe sleeping. "We go out three times a night," I say. "Charlie walks fast for a man his age, barely using his flashlight at all. He knows the route from memory, he says, could do it in his sleep. Sometimes he thinks he does. He's been there twenty-six years. Can you imagine that? Twenty-six years, and now they're canning him. They'll pension him off, I guess. Send him a paycheck until he dies."

"But what will you do?" I'd asked him. "Oh, I don't know. Same old thing, I guess." He'd bent down then, picked up a pebble which glinted in the beam of his flashlight, and threw it with a baseball pitch toward the fence. "Same old thing?" I repeated. "You know, just walking around, watching what goes on about town." I laughed a little at that. "In this town? You won't be seeing very much." "Not a big fan of peace and quiet, are you?" Charlie shot back. "You'd rather live somewhere where there was always muggings and shootings and other exciting things?" Charlie's voice was almost scolding, as if I were a child, and I spat out the first thing that came to mind: "I'd rather live where it rains more than once every two months." "There's plenty of water under this earth, boy. Comfort yourself in that." He referred to the aquifer, I know. It's there, I've seen the things it does, like make the wheat grow when it seems instead that it should burst into flame in the dry heat. But usually it seems no more real than the shimmering mirage of water on asphalt. "They say it's getting old, drying up," I said. Charlie turned suddenly and thrust a hand in my face. With his other hand he clicked the flashlight on, momentarily blinding me. When my eyes focused again, the beam was trained directly on his hand, so closely that the fingers glowed red from the blood under the skin. His hand was nearly fleshless, pinched and cracked, the skin veined and flaky, the nails too shiny and rounded, and a touch of arthritis gave the fingers a clawlike appearance. "See these hands?" he said. "Look at 'em. Looks like they're drying up, don't it? But look close. You can see the blood underneath, can't you? It's still there, ain't it? Still flowing?" Charlie clicked off the flashlight, turned away. "We're not drying up," he said. "Just changing on the outside. Underneath we're still the same." He stalked ahead of me then with his old man's gait: short quick steps, knees bent, shoulders rounded, no looking back.

"But you tell me something now," I say to Martin. "Tell me where you came from." "Hell," Martin says. "I came from Hell's Warehouse." I laugh a little, then curl up on the floor and look at him on the couch. "Johnson was an asshole—" he starts. "No," I stop him. "I don't want to hear about Johnson. Tell me about New York." Now he says no, he says, "Can't you see I'm tired?" And then he walks to the bedroom, mumbling, "Johnson is such a fucker," and I let him go. On the back porch I watch the plant, and the prairie, and somewhere in the distance, I watch the night as well, waiting for its return. Late in the afternoon I join Martin in bed. He's so still he seems to be fading away, and not wanting to disturb him, I leave him, poke a candle in a wax-covered bottle, and sit close to watch it melt into yet another layer of wax, viscous at first, like sludgy water, then brittle, like ice. In one long, softly curved rivulet, I let myself remember the curve of my first lover's face. I say his name aloud: "Henry." The puff of air that escapes my mouth with his name sets the candle flickering, and then, with a sputter, it goes out.

The air conditioner has malfunctioned the second night at work: the guardhouse is freezing and the windows have fogged over. Charlie sits on a wooden stool today, his back bowed. I hadn't noticed a stool in the room yesterday; it must have been shoved under the counter. Charlie looks at the formica surface now, white and barrenly clean except for a lidded cardboard box. "Did you clean up?" I ask. "Not me," he says. "Guess they did it during the day. Put my stuff in that box there." He doesn't turn to me when he talks. "Brrr," I say, and fake a shiver even though he's not watching. "Why don't we go out?" "Not scheduled to go for another hour," Charlie says. "We'll go around twice this time." He finally looks at me. "It's hot as hell out there," he says. "Yeah," I say, "well, it's cold as hell in here." Charlie just nods his head and heaves his weight off the stool, pushes open the door. As I follow him out I squeeze his shoulder, letting my hand linger for just a moment. If he even feels it, he says nothing.

"So what do you do during the day?" I ask. Charlie plods along, slow tonight, silent. "Sleep a little," he finally says, after I've almost forgotten the question. "Sleep a lot now, actually. About five or six hours right after I get home, another couple before I come in for the night." "I can't go to sleep right when I get in. I usually wait a few hours. Too wired up, I guess." This isn't true: I never sleep anymore. "No, no, that's not right," Charlie says quickly, cutting the air with his hand. "You should go straight to sleep when you get home. Otherwise, you'll just be run down and cranky." I sigh, not wanting to get into it. Charlie looks over, and I can see his grin in the pale glow of the plant's lights. "You got a woman?" he asks, and there's a mischievous youthful tone in his voice which I want to preserve. But I answer, "No," and leave it at that. Charlie doesn't. He seems suddenly

animated. "Oh, come on, Johnny boy. You're how old?"
"Twenty," I say. "Twenty," he repeats. "And no woman?
No girlfriend?" For a second I think he stumbles on that,
but then he skips on ahead. "When I was your age I was
already married, me and my wife did it every day. And when
she wasn't around, I always had my hand." My laugh sounds
strained. "Okay, Charlie, I get the picture. But there *are*
other things you can do, you know." We walk on in the
darkness, a quarter mile or so. I hear an isolated dust devil
spinning in the prairie beyond the fence. Farther away, a few
cattle low sleepily, disturbed by the wind or a passing coyote.
But Charlie seems intent only on the ground in front of his
feet and the gravel crunching under his boots. Then his voice
comes, confused: "Are we still talking about your dick?" I
don't answer.

"Hey," he says quickly, and clears his throat. "You live
with your parents maybe?" "No." "Oh. I just thought, you
know, if you were living at home, maybe that's why you
weren't, you know, with any girls." "No, that's not it."
"You write to them?" "What?" I say, not sure what he's
getting at. "Oh. No, I don't write. My parents live here in
town." "See them some, then?" "No, never." Charlie looks
at me briefly. "You live in the same town as them, but not
in the same house, yet you don't go see them or write?" I
sigh. "We had a falling out," I say. Charlie waits three steps.
"Mind if I ask about what?" "They didn't like a friend of
mine." "Look," he says, taking me by the arm. "That's no

reason not to speak to your parents anymore. I mean, surely you can work something out." His hand on my arm squeezes tightly; it doesn't feel like he's squeezing my flesh, though, but something imagined in its place. "That's just not a good reason to break off with your parents," he repeats, letting go of my arm. I think about screaming, but don't. "You tell them that," I say. We're almost back to the guardhouse now, where last night we went inside, poked through paperbacks, listened to the radio, but tonight, with Charlie's things packed in that cardboard box and nothing of my own moved in yet, we'll just hang around and drink coffee, Charlie on his stool, me leaning against a blank glass wall. At the door Charlie turns back to me, holding it closed. "I was just asking because I've got a son, and, well, he's probably a lot older than you, but I never hear from him either. And I've got this feeling he's going to miss me one day, and maybe I'll be dead by then and so what can he do? So just . . ." His voice trails off and his fingers tap the door. "Say something, John. Don't wait that long."

He turns and slowly ascends the guardhouse's two steps. "Hell, the last time I saw him was at his mother's funeral. When people are dead, that's not a good time to get acquainted, you know?" He laughs a little, and turns back to me. "Well, that sure came out funny, didn't it? No matter. You understood me, right?" I nod, not looking at him, thinking, though I try not to, of Henry. Thinking: I understand you, but do you understand me? In the distance I think I see our house and a light shimmering in a window. Just an illusion: the moon glinting off a windowpane, the wetness around my eyes playing tricks with my vision. I swipe at them angrily. "What's the matter?" Charlie asks as I brush past him into the freezing cubicle. "Dust," I say, "it's nothing. Just an old allergy flaring up on me," and I stab at my eyes again.

Martin gasps next to me in his sleep, sucking for air as if he were exhausted, sick, dying. For a brief second I imagine that he is dying, but that fiction, that future, is too empty to contemplate. Unable to sleep when I returned home from work, I jumped around, jittery. I practically forced Martin into making love, and in the end all he did was jerk me off. In the middle of it, looking at me with yellow eyes, he said, "You look terrible. You've got to sleep." I pretended not to hear him, but now I wonder: do I look as bad as he does, as wasted, as washed out? He sleeps under the covers today; his pale body pokes from the green blanket like an ocean-bleached bone covered in seaweed. But then I think, He is my handsomest drowned man, I have cleaned and polished him before, and I will do so again.

"Martin," I whisper in his white seashell of an ear. "Wake up." He is completely without reaction, not speaking, not moving, not even breathing differently. "Martin," I repeat, louder this time, and tap his shoulder. "Wake up. I want to talk to you." He moves this time, only a little, but I sigh with relief. "Come on," I call loudly. He doesn't really react, but his breathing has altered. "Please," I whine. "I can't sleep. I haven't slept for days. It's driving me crazy." Suddenly I really am worried about myself, and I jump out of bed, flip on the light, run to a small mirror on the wall. My eyes are bloodshot and circled with dark rings. My lips are cracked and seem slightly swollen. I've forgotten to shave since the job started, and my beard has come in shabbily, in patches. That's all I can see of myself in the mirror, the tiny square of my face, and it seems masklike, a mask which, in its decrepitude, seems to accurately project what lies underneath. "Martin!" I call.

And his hands are on my shoulders, soothing, cool. I turn and hug him desperately. It's all right, he says. In the large mirror over the dresser I can see only my face and arms wrapped around his sheet-draped body. In the farther mirror I don't look as bad: a little pale, somewhat unkempt. Disheveled. As though I'd just had sex. And then, remembering the first image, my cracked lips and sunken eyes, I add a mental note: in a desert. I let go of Martin and rush over to a small bookcase. We'd hollowed out a copy of *Gulliver's Travels*, thinking it somehow appropriate, and from within its bindings I dump our savings. A pile of bills and a few coins fall to the floor. I'd told him keeping the money in a book was a romantic thing to do; now I see it as the work of a siege mentality: keep what you need close to home, in case you must flee. "Let's go," I say. "Right now. Let's just go."

Martin comes to me, letting the sheet slip from his body. The hair on his stomach is sticky and clumped together from where I'd come on him a little while ago, and though I wish him silent, he speaks. "We can't leave, John," he says, gathering up the money. "You know there's not enough here." He has the money in both hands; the bills poke from his fingers like leaves. There are barely seven hundred dollars there. We were able to buy the house on a loan two years ago, and the payments keep the pile small. He called the house an investment when we first talked of buying it, saying it would increase in value and, with the selling of it, finance our move to New York. But, seeing him with that skimpy wad of money in his hands, like leaves, I realize that one doesn't buy a house in order to leave it. Martin *is* like a tree, a tree of the prairie; he wants only to grow in one place, and drink what little there is.

I swat the money from his hands. I squat down like a child. "There's lots here," I say, and indeed, it looks like a lot, since we've never bothered to exchange the ones and fives for tens and twenties. Looking up at him, I'm at eye level with his penis. "There's lots we could do with this," I say. Martin kneels beside me. "John," he says quietly, "this wouldn't even pay for our plane tickets." "Then forget about the plane tickets. Pretend we're already there." He asks what I mean. "A game, Martin, let's play a game." I settle on the floor, sitting Indian-style. "We're in New York, see, and we've got all this money in our pockets." Martin sits back against the bedroom wall and closes his eyes. With the loss of their tiny spots of color, his white frame seems to melt into the wall. "Please, John, I'm not in the mood for pretend games. I'm tired of talking about New York. It makes me sick." "No, Martin, please." I put my fingers on his mouth, silencing him. "I need to keep this one story going, okay? It means a lot to me." He opens his eyes. "It means too much to you, John." "No, no, not too much. You don't understand, Martin. This New York, it's the only story I believe in any-more. All those other stories, the ones they teach you growing up, I gave those up years ago. But this one I need. I need to have at least one story." Martin takes my hand from his chin, holds it in his. "John, come on, you don't need stories. That's why I'm here." I look at him, confused, staring full on into the bottomless tranquillity of his eyes. What's in there that makes him say that? "I'm not saying I should be your whole life," he continues, "just that I'm here. There's more I can offer you than just stories about New York." "Henry said something like that once. Said he could give me more than my mother ever could." Martin's voice, when it comes, is disgusted. "Henry was an old lech who took advantage of a little kid." "I *loved* Henry!" I yell. Then, in a quieter voice: "God, I remember being with him. He was so gentle. It didn't matter how often we did it, he'd always treat me like it was my first time. He went so slow, so kind. It almost felt like my first time, you know, each time. No one's ever done that for me since." I look up, startled. "I guess that means

you." Martin sighs. "John, you were thirteen. Your pubic
hair still feels new at thirteen."

Henry, my first lover, was gray-haired and fleshy, a kind
man run out of town because here they can still do that,
rather than use the courts or jail. Here, they can fire someone
from his job, not cash his checks, not sell him food from the
only grocery store in town. And of course the town didn't
single out just Henry, but Martin refuses to understand that.
I thought I could sleep with him just once. I used to sneak
over there nearly every night. Henry wasn't old, but he'd
reached a point, I think, where sex tired him out more than
when you're young. And I'd worked hard that night, got him
to do it twice, so he was exhausted, and then I lay with him
until he fell asleep, telling him all the while I'd leave. And
when he fell asleep, I curled up next to him, my face right
in his, so I could feel his breath on my skin, and I went to
sleep. The next thing I knew, my parents were there, and
the sheriff, and Henry's neighbor, who'd seen me coming
and going. I don't remember what they said, and I don't
remember them actually hitting me. I just remember Henry
yelling, I told you not to fall asleep! And I started to say I
was sorry, but someone put a hand over my mouth, so he
never learned that. He left soon after. I remember seeing
him once or twice more. I never approached him. He'd have
run from me, I think; I'd probably have run from him. He
looked scared, hunted. His face sagged, his stomach had
swelled. In weeks, he'd grown old. Years later I'd wanted to

call him, tell him I'd at last met someone else: Martin. But instead, I got in a fight with my parents and they announced, their trump card, making them winners despite the fact that it had nothing to do with anything, By the way, Henry's dead. Dropped off like a bug in winter. Heart disease, or some such.

Martin is stacking the money into neat piles when I look up. I watch him until he's finished. He looks at me. "Okay, we're there. We have seven hundred and twenty dollars. We can do anything you want." He pauses. "John, I'm sorry. I had no idea." "How could you? I never told you." Martin starts to say something, then stops, and then we rent a hotel room: a hundred dollars. We go shopping: Martin shows me where to go for cheap used clothing, which sidewalks are okay to shop from, which are rip-offs. One day stretches into two, and there is another night's rent, and meals, most cheap, but a couple of more pricey ones in midtown. When only a small pile of unspent money is left, I suggest we go to a concert. Martin smiles and says the name of a bar. Maxwell's, in Hoboken. "It'll be cheaper that way," he says, "and it'll give us a chance to get out of the city." "But we just got here." He pulls out two dollars in quarters from the small pile of change. "For the PATH," he says, "it's like the subway to Jersey." Then he pulls out ten dollars each for ticket money. "We'll think cheap. A local band is playing tonight." We have a couple of beers at Maxwell's, more money. The concert is good, really loud, and toward the end the back room of the bar gets raucous with dancing people bouncing off each other. We slip out just before the end of the first encore. "Oh!" I cry, "but it's gotten dark and cold in Hoboken, New Jersey, and it's raining cats and dogs. We get to walk in the rain!" "Ah!" Martin exclaims, smiling, "but there's a gypsy cab right here, to whisk us back to the train station in warmth and speed!" "And to use up the rest of our dollar bills," I say, holding up four wrinkled singles. There's only a loose pile of change on the floor now. "It's okay," Martin tells me, saying he paid for an extra night at the hotel; all we have to do is get back. He smiles wickedly. "And then your ass is *mine*." "And we have just enough to do it," I say. "A dollar for you"—I count out four quarters—"and a dollar for me," I add, taking the last coins, two quarters and a half-dollar. "Wait." Martin stops me. "What's that?" "This? It's just a half-dollar." "But the PATH machines don't take them. You should've changed it." "What do you mean, I should've changed it? I don't know the first thing about those machines. Let's change it now." He slumps against the wall and pulls the sheet across his lap. "But it's late, nothing's open." "So what does that mean?" "It means we're stuck." "We're stuck in Hoboken?" Martin laughs a little. "In the cold and the dark and the rain," he says. "Yes," I say. I remember, it was I who made it rain.

"I *told* you," he tells me, sounding like a angry child. "If we'd had more money we could've taken the taxi back to Manhattan." I pick up the money, stuff it back in the book, and put it all back on the shelf. I want to ask him why he didn't say something, warn me. But I'm afraid he'll say, Why didn't you tell me about Henry? And I want to ask him again, Where did you come from, why did you come here? but I have no idea what he'd say to that. When I turn off the light, I realize it's fully dark out. Time to get up.

I walk the two miles home from my third day of work slowly, my feet sweating in the heavy boots. Small clouds of dust puff up with each footfall, and I watch these to avoid staring at the vehicles which race past me on the highway. I'm almost home when I look up and see our house: it sits isolated, a half mile from town, and behind it, the just-risen sun glows, illuminating the paint so that it seems yellow, almost golden. The windows are open and a breeze blowing through the house flutters the curtains outside the sills; as I approach they wave at me, or perhaps they warn me away. I take my boots off before I go inside and wipe my feet with the dry tops of my socks. I enter the house quietly in case Martin is sleeping on the couch. He's not. I see him sitting at the kitchen table in his white work clothes; he isn't moving at the table and doesn't seem to have noticed me. I unbutton and remove my sweaty shirt, then walk into the kitchen. Martin perches on the chair with shoulders hunched, back slumped, head leaning forward. On the table a cup of instant soup steams in a clear glass mug. Martin doesn't look up when I greet him, and I notice that his chin and shirt are stained with broth and a whitish-yellow noodle clings to his face just below his lip.

"Johnson was on my case again last night. Faggot this, faggot that." His voice startles me. "I'm sorry," I say, and go to the cabinets, grabbing a cup and a package of soup. I turn the gas on under the teakettle. Martin idly twirls the spoon around in the soup. "He said, I heard you're living with that Italian boy, what's-his-name. Everyone *knows* he's a faggot. I said, So what? He said, So he's a *faggot*." His voice inflects slightly, but something in his tone brings out the vehemence, the hatred. Only, I can't tell if he's imitating Johnson's or if it's his own. I don't know if I should go to him or stay back. I don't know what to do in a situation like this; I've never been in a situation like this before. "I got mad, I guess. I said, So what if he's a faggot? What if I'm a faggot? He said, Then I'm going to run you out of town on a rail." His head turns as he says this. His lips twist, half-snarl, half-cry, and his cheeks turn red. Then, as quickly as it started, his face relaxes, and he just sits there again. What does that mean, I wonder, on a rail? The teakettle whistles that my water is boiling. I empty the yellow powder and dried noodles from the soup package into my cup and lift the kettle from the stove. "What happened?" I ask. "He made me blow him or else he'd fire me." The water gushes from the kettle's spout too quickly and some of the soup splashes on the counter. I stir it a little, my spoon clinking against the sides of the mug, then I set the spoon on the counter and place the kettle on top of the cup so the dehydrated noodles will steep and become soft and fleshy. It takes a few minutes, a little time, for the absorption to take place. I wish I could rush it, but I can't.

I take Martin from behind, encircle his chest with my arms. Looking down the slope of his face, I see the noodle clinging below his lip and I reach up and remove it. Martin takes small sloppy bites of his soup. His cheeks are red again, but he isn't crying. I say, "We'll leave soon." Martin says, "Never get angry." I let go of him. "I've got to go take a shower." When I'm in the bathroom I think I hear his voice in the other room. I don't ask him what he said. Instead I call out, "Charlie invited us to dinner," and turn on the bathtub water. "Do you want to go, Martin? There'll be plenty to eat." There's a pause, and then I hear Martin sing-songing, "Charlie, Charlie, Charlie, Charlie." "What about Charlie?" I call. If he answers me, I don't hear him. All I hear is the hissing of the shower and a low gurgle as water leaks down the drain.

Between bites of doughnut, Charlie'd said, "You know we're useless, don't you, kid?" "What?" "Twenty-six years I been here. That's a quarter century plus. And in all that time there's never been one break-in, not even an attempted break-in. Not into any of the offices, not the safe, and certainly nothing having to do with national security wrenches." "What are you talking about, Charlie?" "Hell, they're just Allen wrenches anyway. This whole shebang was just some old senator's gift to his home state back in the fifties. He guaranteed them defense jobs, see, and they guaranteed him votes. And this night watchman's job, it's just one more useless job that goes along with this whole useless plant." He paused, then pushed on. "We're not the only night watchmen, you know?" "No, I—" "There was another one, before me. But he's dead now, no wife, no family, nothing left behind him. Sometimes I think I'm the only one that even knows he existed. But it's okay, I guess, however you touch other people, as long as you touch them, understand them a little, it's okay."

Dinner at Charlie's, once it's cooked, is a short affair. Martin eats little, but drinks three beers quickly, biting his lips and frowning. Charlie and I talk loudly around him, and eat all the food that he doesn't. Once, Charlie asks Martin if he's feeling okay, but I answer for him. "Just tired," I say. "He's just tired. He works a night shift too." "Yeah?" Charlie says. "My wife used to work a night shift for a while, so we could spend more time together." "What a coincidence," Martin says, speaking for the first time. Charlie looks at Martin chewing on his lips. "Everything taste okay to you, son?" "Everything's fine," Martin says, then turns to look at me. "Everything's just like John said it would be." "What?" I say. "I didn't say anything." Martin harrumphs. "Well," Charlie says quickly, "if you're not going to eat this, I'll just help myself," and he reaches to Martin's plate and takes a chicken leg that's only been nibbled on. And then dinner's over. On the way out, I say to Charlie, "Are you sure we can't help you clean up or something?" "No, no," Charlie says, cleaning his teeth with a toothpick. "I'll get it." "Do you want to sit outside for a while? We could," and here I pause, thinking of what to do. "We could watch the night or something, the stars." "No, that's okay. Think I'll just do the dishes and go to bed. You two probably want to get home anyway." "Well, look," I say, conscious of Martin walking away from me. "If there's anything I can do for you, anything at all, you be sure and give me a call, okay?" Charlie looks flustered, almost embarrassed. "Look, son," he says, and I feel that he's embarrassed for me, not himself. "If there's anyone you should be taking care of, it's Martin."

Now there's just the two of us walking home, a couple of feet apart on the sidewalk. It's early evening, the time of the day when the black starry bowl of the sky drops down like a cool blanket to soothe the earth's charred skin. Soon enough, though, like a real blanket in summer, the coolness is gone, leaving only hot scratchy fabric to grate over our skin. "You want to hear something about New York, John?" Martin says to me. I have a feeling I don't, but I keep silent. "I went to a party once, I was sixteen. There was this man playing the piano. He was beautiful. He sat at the piano as if he'd had nothing better to do all his life than sit at pianos and entertain people. And then this other man comes up. He was around

DALE PECK

the same age, but he seemed younger, more insecure. He gives the first man a drink, and then they start talking, and it's obvious that there's a seduction going on. I mean, just the way that guy played, so quietly, smiling, laughing every once in a while. And the second guy slides on the bench and they sit together for a while, the first man playing, the second one turning the pages of the sheet music, and then, after a while, they get up and leave together, and you just know what they're going to do." He's spoken quietly but quickly, and it seems we've not traveled very far since the beginning of the story. "I don't understand what that's got to do with us," I say. Martin plunges ahead, his voice desperate. "That party, John, that guy, so cool, so suave. The two of them went together so well. You could see them falling in love, right there, in their own little world, you could tell nothing was going to go wrong in their lives. I didn't just want to take the other guy's place, John, I wanted to *be* him." "I still don't get it," I say, feeling stupid. "You don't get it?" he practically shouts at me, and I look around nervously. He grabs me by the hand and I have to resist the urge to pull free. "You don't get it? Well, get this: I wanted us to be them. When I came out here, and out of the blue met you, I thought, This is it. *We're* it. We're them." He lets go of my hand and I'm relieved. I say, "But it hasn't turned out like that. For you." We're almost at the house now. We turn up the path and the walk seems immensely long, a thin spindly bridge across a chasm that we can only traverse single-file. I watch Martin's hunched shrinking shoulders as he ascends the porch steps. His white back is ghostlike, almost transparent as he walks under the shadow of the porch. He opens the door to the house, turns to me. He's licking his lips with an expression of distaste. "No," he says, "it hasn't."

I walk in behind him, then go to a window and see the plant in the slit between the two curtains. "I'm going to stay up for a while," I say. At this distance, the plant seems as small and insignificant under the sky as I am. "John," Martin's voice calls from the other room, "are you coming to bed or not?" "Soon," I call. "Soon." Sometimes I think that, given other choices, Martin and I wouldn't have come together at all. I used to feel sure that whatever we were missing would appear somewhere, someday, perhaps lying beside the road or out in the open fields. Perhaps I'll look up on my walk home from work and glean something from the brown-gold light of the sunrise that so resembles the dying light of sunset: it *will* be there, I tell myself, whatever it is. Until then, there is Martin; for a time, he will do, and, I suppose, I do for him. Such, I guess, such is the gaseous nature of love, which expands to fill whatever shape encompasses it.

I open the curtains wide—something we never do when we're home—and push up the glass. It's big and empty out there, quiet, and it seems like now there's nothing to keep out of the room, and, as well, nothing to keep in.

THE END OF THE

OCEAN

I

"Love is in the morning," he said, "after a long night spent sleeping together." We sat at his table. Eggs steamed the air before us, a bottle of milk waited to fill empty glasses. "Why the morning?" I asked. "Because in the morning," he said, "you're just awake." He yawned and then smiled, as if at a joke I wasn't getting. "Just awake?" I asked. "What does that mean? And anyway, shouldn't love be at night, in bed?" He just smiled, then poured milk in his glass without looking at it and handed the bottle to me. "Why not at night?" I repeated. Last night we'd met, talked, come here, had sex, fallen asleep: if love existed, wasn't that the place to look for it? And then I remembered dreams, interrupted, awakened by his hands, as he'd taken me a second time and I pretended to sleep. Now, pouring milk in my glass, I watched him, spilled a little, and handed the bottle back to him. He stood up then, so close to me that the white plain of his stomach filled my vision and the odor of his crotch filled my nose. I leaned my head toward it, my mouth already open: I thought that's what *he wanted. But he pushed me back, walked behind me, behind my chair. He held me then kissed me then ran the cold milk bottle between my legs, and then, "John," he said, "this is not just love, nor is it all of love." He held up the half-drunk bottle and swirled the milk in it, and then he put it on the table and ran his wet hand down my back. He stopped at the base, scratched me lightly. I shivered as cold water ran off my thighs, and then I turned in my chair and put my hand, my big clumsy hand, on his chest. Each finger took a rib like shipwrecked swimmers clutching at life rafts, but my thumb danced over his heart, alone, uncertain. And then I gave in and moved close. I rested my ear against his chest, encircled him with my arms, and lay like a swimmer who has at last reached the end of the ocean. "Love is in the morning," Martin repeated, mouthing the words into my ear, kissing it with dry lips, moving his wet hand up and down my back, making me, making me want . . . nothing. "After a long night spent sleeping together." Beneath my ear, his heart moved a river of blood on its way and, at the thought of that, part of me shivered, and part of me was warm.*

ALWAYS AND

FOREVER

∎

> They saw a couple of drawings that I had
> made of the establishment, and Mrs.
> Monarch hinted that it never would have
> struck her that he had sat for them.
> "Now the drawings you make from us, they
> look exactly like us," she reminded me,
> smiling in triumph; and I recognized
> that this was indeed just their defect.
> —Henry James, "The Real Thing"

I have known Martin for two and a half months, and this apartment, formerly his alone, still feels new. Sometimes I read Martin's journal. It's written in a compact precise hand distinguished from anything else he writes, which sprawls illegibly all over the place. Martin is a writer, though he's never tried to publish. His story, a long, perhaps unending narrative, floats at me from off the page, defying the cramped letters that frame it, spilling out into life. There is much of

Martin in it; there are things I hadn't thought of before, but after reading him, I ask myself, Is this real? and then answer, Yes. The words often seem spoken by children, or adults so close to their childhood that it still breaks over them in waves. Martin acts like a child, wild, impulsive, and carefree. He drops money on whims: gifts for me or old lovers whose friendship he still covets, or for other friends. He's compulsive about his gift-giving, his goodwill; at his most rash I've seen him walk the city blocks with hundreds of dollar bills rolled in a ball and stuffed into one of the deep pockets of his pants. At every outstretched hand or cup he peels off a dollar, and into the receptacle, like a piece of food, he places the money, a gift of nourishment. Some people say he wastes these dollars, but Martin has plenty of money to give—perhaps even more than he has compassion. Martin wants to connect with the world. That's a phrase that appears in his journal. It's what the money means when he gives it away, and other things he does, like teach school, are all part of this desire to connect. Martin loves children, but is afraid of scandal or invasion by prying eyes if he tries to adopt. So he teaches grade school weekdays, and while he's gone I do things about the house and run errands, visit my friends or shop, waiting for him to come home. It's easy to love Martin: he's rich, nice-looking, has a remarkably affectionate personality, and he loves me. He loves like a child, and I guess, despite my outlook on life, so do I. The closer I get to him the younger I feel, more impulsive and, strangely, more in control of myself, as though I'm free to visit a different world, one that Martin brings to me. Sometimes when I read Martin's journal and taste his little snatches of story, see his bright bursts of color and imagination, I feel this way, and feel also a rush of love, just from his words.

I'll always remember his chain of flowers. Originally, I must have noticed all the flowers in the apartment as vague scenery when we first made love. They were arranged haphazardly, spilling out of broad fat vases everywhere. I thought of these while I read about Martin's chain; in his story he rolled the world into a clay ball and then stretched it out into a long, snaky coil tendriled in thousands of budded offshoots. The flowers emerged in yellow, lavender, orange, and blue balls, in long green or milky-white stems, in occasional leaves that hang like forgotten dancers in a corner but, when turned over, yield their own beauty: a lace-like webbing of veins that pucker the undersides of the leaves with their finely wrought patterns. This is the chain, the great thick chain, wound as thickly as a ship's anchor rope, so strong that human beings can climb on it. In Martin's story, only the children do. The adults pass by, ignoring its beauty, but when they go home perhaps they notice for the first time the dandelions that force their way through cracks in the sidewalk, and are reminded of some time from their past, Christmas or a birthday, of little bits of wrapping paper dotting a wooden floor with spots of color and remembered goodwill. I tease Martin when he says there are flowers everywhere, flowers are the links on the great chain of being. I call him my flower child, at which he blushes, and his flushed pale skin resembles nothing so much as a pink-tinted carnation.

We met at a friend's party. Martin, I learned, was frequently a guest at Sue's because he always hit it off with everyone: all the men and women chased him, but he always left alone. This was my first time at her place. I was new to the city and I was surprised when she pointed him out to me, told me she'd invited me with him in mind. He attracted attention as a peacock does, spectators gathering to await the unfurling of magnificent tail feathers. For Martin nothing so spectacular was required: he could play the piano and sing so that the most masculine-looking men rolled their eyes heavenward like queens, and the women leaned to one another and whispered, "Oh, if only." Sue told me all this.

I approached him tentatively. Actually, Sue dragged me from a corner and sent me over with a drink for him, a tropical specialty of hers whose colored silhouette shifted in the glass in bands of mauve and orange and clear dark rum before they swirled together. Martin took it from me with thanks and, before I knew it, was talking to me quietly. Like everyone else, I was captivated, and answered his questions as best I could, trying not to look doe-eyed. Dancing on the piano in front of him, a terra-cotta horse bowed its head under the heavy weight of its rider. Martin noticed me looking at it. "Do you ride?" he asked, still playing. I told him I hadn't ridden since childhood. His words, fitted between the notes he pressed from the piano keys, "Why did you stop?" seemed to come only to me, while the music slipped past us to the people dispersed throughout the room. I remembered the horse I had learned to ride on when I was young, an older gelding, peaceful and stalwart, the ideal mount for a nervous rider like myself. I said, "The horse I rode died."

"Do you know Bartók?" Martin asked me. "No," I said, surprised, and Martin drifted gently from what he had been playing into a song I'd never heard; I assumed it was Bartók. "Tell me how it died." "Well," I said, and then I was off, remembering. Once, I arrived at the stable and someone else sat on the horse, riding next to one of the stallions kept there. The person repeatedly cropped the gelding's gray back. I remember the horse frothing in discomfort and shredding the earth with dancing steps. And then, almost exactly as they passed in front of me, the rider brought the whip down hard across the gelding's face.

The passage came to an end; without faltering, Martin began another, his eyes fixed on the ashen lines of the horse before him. "Vivaldi," he said. " 'Autumn.' " I went on. It was too late after that to do anything: the horse reared back, and its eyes were ringed with this vivid white line, and it exploded into fury, turning not on its assailant but on the stallion. Both riders lost their seats in the battle and were nearly trammeled by the wild hooves. The gelding's rage added strength and some kind of blind skill to its attack, but in the end the stallion crushed it underfoot and stood on it in triumph, his black coat bleeding on the gelding's destroyed form, and all the while the stable hands and I looked on helplessly.

And another song ended. Martin took his hands from the keys to pick up the horse. "Thousands of these were found in a Chinese emperor's tomb," he said. "They were his soldiers, meant to guard him on his way to the next world. They were arrayed around his sarcophagus like a miniature army, a tiny, stationary, but perfectly created world." He paused and then said, "We had horses when I was young." He looked at me, smiled; his eyes seemed vacant. "Nothing so spectacular happened when I was growing up," he nearly whispered, then looked back at the horse in his lap. The silence between us made others notice; some turned to look. A voice called for more music. "Well," he said, replacing the statue after a moment's hesitation, "what shall I play now?" and he patted the bench next to him with his right hand, opened the sheet music on the piano with his left. "Would you turn pages for me?"

Sometime later in the evening—and this was just fortuitous, pure luck—I left my seat and pulled a rose from a jade vase and, returning to his side, bit off the stem and placed the half-open flower in his lapel buttonhole as he sat at the piano. His hands slowed; he improvised on the song he was playing and they drifted up to the higher keys, tolling out long, bell-like chimes. He sniffed the flower with closed eyes, then returned to his song. Later he approached me, the rose bleeding on his black jacket, and asked me if I wanted to go dancing. We slipped out, he first sharing something with Sue and pointing at me where I stood by the door, and then we were off, to the Cat Club. Once there, his gentleness disappeared in a gradually quickening twisting of his body. Even as we stood on line for the entrance, he began snapping his fingers quietly, quickly, in apparently random patterns, until I could hear the music more clearly, and could tell he was picking out riffs and trills, not just the beat. His eyes widened and sparkled, his feet tamped in place. Inside, he swam through the dark crowd like an eel, and I followed as he peeled off his coat and laid it over a chair, lifted the rose from the buttonhole and smelled it, replaced it. Then he was on the floor, and his feet began shuffling rapidly and his arms lifted from his body like a ballet dancer's. Soon he was moving with graceful abandon, lip-syncing and grinding his body, occasionally dancing in close to me but generally apart, in a space that was soon yielded to his flailing arms and backward, forward, circular gait. I don't know if he danced separately from me because he felt nervous about being half of the only gay couple in a straight club or if, as seemed natural, he preferred to move freely. At any rate, I, like the rest of the club, was a curious spectator of Martin's ferocity. At one point the DJ was playing an intense punk tune, and Martin's dancing, almost out of control, seemed more like convulsing than rhythmic movement. I moved away, confused, a little frightened: an onlooker. He rolled his head back once and I saw his eyes: black impenetrable depths in the off-light, so wide now that a white line showed around the iris. Their blank gaze zeroed in on me once, and then, stomping, he turned away.

Through the masked expressions worn while we made love —lips furled exposing half-open mouths, sharp teeth; eyes open and vacant, or closed and strangely focused; skin covered in creeping red tones—I remembered Martin dancing. With sex there was no hint of the frenzy I had seen on the dance floor. Martin made love as, I imagine, a precocious pre-adolescent imagines it, slowly and tenderly, with an emphasis placed on total body pleasure, so that our final genital orgasms seemed merely a soft finale to the entire act. He lit small, many-colored candles for effect, burned amber cones of incense in each room, and made love to me throughout his apartment, as if conducting me on a dizzying private tour, which is when I noticed the flowers everywhere. But we finished finally on his bed, where we made love on sheets the color and softness of corn silk, not quite recklessly, but still ardently; the condoms, like everything else he used, were in bright colors: blue and green, yellow and orange.

He wooed me with a modern courtesan's ploys for the next

month: with flowers delivered daily, with notes Fed Ex'd to me when I visited my parents in Kansas for four days. With gifts: a few items of clothing, a new camera so that I could further my photography. With travels: a trip to Paris when I returned, and one to Jamaica the day after the first snowfall, where we lolled indolently upon the white-glass beaches and thought of the snow at home, still white when we'd flown out of JFK that morning. Then one day, four weeks after I met him, I entered his apartment with my bronze key, which still bore the scratches from its recent cutting, and he clucked and crowed like a preening rooster, and led me to what had been a closet, showing me a newly installed darkroom, telling me I could use it as often as I liked day or night, even if I didn't want to move in just yet. I moved in. He tempered his romance then, slowly, over the next weeks. It was a maturity, though we still spoke with the words of child lovers. This was our highest moment: on the far stretch of a beach in Jamaica—our second trip there—he rolled on top of me and kissed my lips. I remember him saying, "I love you, I will always love you." The sun shone on his back and filtered through his hair into my eyes. Far away from us, men slipped surreptitiously over an invisible but undeniable line of seg-regation at the beach, and I remembered once seeing two men kiss in the rainy street below the amber-shaded windows of Martin's apartment. Martin's face was a blur, too shad-owed, too close to mine for me to see it clearly, and his words fell into my ears like the sweat rolling off his nose. "And I," I said, "I shall love you forever."

It's strange not to have to work. I have time to indulge myself, time to waste, time to dig through Martin's journal like an archaeologist exploring a past life. I sometimes think that, like Martin, I'll take a job that I enjoy, but I haven't picked one yet, and Martin sees no reason why I should rush into anything. So I take a lot of pictures, roaming the city, first a tourist, later a resident, and just recently I try to look at it as a stranger with self-created expectations. I've made hundreds of prints, thrown most away. When I take pictures they come out stark; I remember trying to make the city more beautiful than it actually was when I held the camera, but to do that I had to cut out the people and the ground, the grimy colors, the filth, and so I have a pile of overexposed blanched white-on-gray pictures of the tops of buildings jutting into an unreceiving sky. They seem not so much pretty as empty and colorless; the clouds are just a skullcap to cover their baldness, and as I file them away, I think that I still have much to learn about technique, about lenses, about ways of viewing the world.

So I visited him where he teaches. I made a pretext of bringing him some papers he left at home, but really I only wanted to see him teach, see where he works and meet his children, whom I have heard of only through scattered commentary. The room stood empty when I found it through the maze of hallways; it was near noon, so I assumed they were all at lunch. I walked in and looked around. The classroom seemed like any other in the city, at first. One wall had a row of windows, some panes frosted, others tinted, most dirty on the outside, so that the view was ever-changing as I walked down the length of the room. Two other walls were short, flat, and inconsequential—the two with blackboards. The final wall, opposite the windows, was covered by corkboard, the corkboard by paper. I walked to it, skirting the circles of many-colored desks clumped in the room like flowers. It was hard to see the children's things clearly on the bulletin board, because the sun at my back cast a shadow directly where I wanted to look. Martin had mentioned to me that he simply let the students put up what they liked best: sometimes it was a poem written about the sun's clarity, or pictures they'd drawn or finger-painted, always greens, blues, and yellows—light, cheerful tones in patterns like rainbows extracted from oil on water. I remember in particular one girl's work. She had beautiful childish handwriting, and all she displayed were her penmanship papers. Just words written over and over—apple tree, apple tree, apple tree; brook, brook, brook; mother, mother, mother—all scrolled with a flourishing prosody. This, I learned at home when I asked Martin about her, after I had seen him teaching in his mask of smiles, soft words, and exaggerated gestures, gave a visible appearance to those objects she had never seen.

*   *   *

Behind the north wall of Martin's apartment another building lingers: old, unused, and dirty. A large window in the den breaks on it, but the blind, painted with an Arabic pattern, is always drawn. It is in the den that Martin writes, with his back to the blind, so he can look out the room's other window and see the river. Through the semi-clear shade the dirty water of the Hudson and, beyond it, New Jersey, turn golden and beautiful. What is he writing about? I wonder as I read through his pages. Just flowers? Just beauty and elegance and eloquence, of his own personal view of perfection? He's told me imagination is like gathering the colored strands of the rainbow and braiding them together into white light. I imagine it: sometimes he sits at the back of a man—me?—with long, many-colored hair and weaves his braid; sometimes he's a puppet suspended on seven different-colored strings, struggling until the strings tangle into a thick hanging chain. This isn't a story, some would say, because there is no conflict within it; this is an account, long and flawless, multifaceted like a jewel, but forever the same thing. But when Martin puts down his pen, closes his book, leaves the den, I follow him through the rooms until he finds a place to sit down, raise the shade, and look out at the city; when that happens, I see him gaze at the pollution, the disarrayed lights like stars all out of kilter, the mad dashing of those who don't move within his ordered world, ever, and I know what he writes about, why it is a story. No, he said to me when I asked him if I could read his journal. This isn't real. Its conflict is with reality. So I go to him after he writes and wait for a while, then close the blinds, light the candles and the incense, show him his flowers, make love to him, and give him his fiction, because I need it too.

In a revealing moment—and Martin has many of these, but I mean the ones when he is speaking—Martin admitted to me that he's terrified of the world. "Why?" I asked. He said he would live, if he could, with his back pressed up against the farthest corner of everything so that he could see someone coming for him and run. "Why?" I asked again. He turned his face from me and mumbled something about not liking to talk about it. We sat on the thick carpet in an alcove of the long tunnel of the living room, our backs pressed against the plush of the couch, amber-tinted sunlight wrapping itself around our unclothed bodies. Steam from mugs of tea made our brows damp; with a hand warmed from the porcelain I touched him on the shoulder, cheek, lips, as if my heat could thaw him, open his mouth, let him release himself. "Why?" I asked a third time. In an almost violent flood, he turned to me and said, "The world only needs to hit you once and you'll never trust it again."

I sat back, asked him what he meant. He turned his open body to me. I touched it, experimentally. His reddening skin was like rubber under my fingers and didn't respond. "When I was much younger, we lived in Maine," he said. "My father was still alive, and he'd married my stepmother by then. We

lived at the Park." His eyes went wide, and I saw him remember the place. His ancestral home, he's called it: palatial,
marble, cold, gray, hemmed in all around by severely clipped
green-black boxwood hedges. "I came home with a new hair-
cut once—I was fifteen or sixteen—and my father got very
upset. He decried it practically, as though it were bad diplo-
macy on my part. He called it hippie, womanly, faggotty."
Martin drew his arms and legs in close, as though it were
cold in the room. I stretched him out again silently, as though
to say, Feel the air: in here, it's always warm. "But then he
began insulting me with things that didn't offend me but him
as well. Profanity, like I'd never heard him use, for hours on
end. Shithead, mother—" "No." I stopped him. "You don't
have to use his words." Cut off, he looked at me. The cold
was only in his eyes by then, which were stretched open, the
lids almost propped apart beyond their means. "Finally I
escaped to bed. But late in the night he dragged me to the
living room. Beatrice was there, sitting in a leather chair,
wearing a sequined gown, holding a glass by the tips of her
fingernails. She looked like an ice cube in rum. My father
was drunk but steady on his feet. She just watched. He
smacked me open-palmed, so the noise was like hands clap-
ping, and he went on and on about my insolence, auda-
ciousness, and disrespect for his parental authority, and his
slaps sounded like an audience cheering him on. I was so
stunned I didn't react, and then my father punched me, hard,
again and again, in the face and body. I would fall and he'd

wait for me to stand up, and hit me down again. I didn't say anything. I remember seeing for the first time blood on my face in the mirror over the fireplace." I imagined him: so caught up in the image that he lost his father, forgot the beating, saw only the red spilling over newly formed dark stubble on his chin, sliding quickly down his black pajamas. I could see him as a teenager as I held him then, trying to warm him, nine years later: his body blossoming with late adolescence, with his first pangs of sexual desire, with the blood like a wave of heat washing over him, warming even his feet on the cold stone floor. "And then I heard my father scream, and it seemed to me he'd left reality"—but I know: the scream was the real world—"'I'll teach you to ignore me! I saw it first, swinging like a bat toward my head. A log taken from beside the fireplace, a pine branch which still had some dried pale green needles on it, even one tiny pinecone. I remember thinking, We burn pine so the resin in it will pop and explode in golden fountains of sparks and make the fire even more beautiful. And then my head exploded, and I was knocked unconscious."

How far away, I thought, are these stretched-out limbs from those of the boy years ago? His left leg twitched, and I quieted it with my hand, waiting for him to finish. "Even at the hospital there was no solace. My stepmother volunteered there, my father gave money. No one questioned their story. I was mugged, they said, and my jaw was wired shut so I couldn't contradict them, even though I wanted to. Then we rode home, and in the limo my father told me: This could happen anytime, if I didn't pay him heed." As warm as we were then, in the little sheltered cove of his living room, I could still see him. Huddled on the long seat in the stifling black pod of the limousine, perhaps some blood still slipping out between barely opened lips, cold wire poking his cheek. And his father's warning: This would happen anytime, anytime. "And the thing is," Martin explained to me, "it doesn't have to happen over and over. My father never hit me again, and he apologized profusely for months afterward. It doesn't have to be a horror story. It only has to happen once." He trembled when he finished, and I thought, Once, only once? "No, Martin," I said aloud. "Not only once." But his body begged to be held like a baby's; he couldn't speak, so we held each other, like twins.

Yesterday Martin and I attended a funeral. Though my first, it was just another in a progression for the other men; for a few, it was a brief encounter with their own. We were, in a way, lucky, for there was no grieving lover, no one to lose control and offer useless bargains with death and, worse, to feel the undeserved guilt of a murderer or the unknowing betrayal of the murdered. There was none of that there, just friends to stand in for the last vigil in somber clothing. They were silent; by now they had become inured to words, even their own. At such moments they have strength only to wait for this to pass, in whatever manner it chooses. Martin had sent over a vanload of flowers, and they spilled in wreaths over the naked pile of clay soil with the light unemotional colors of sympathy. The softly painted flowers of Martin's tie, almost lost inside his black suit, seemed the only thing about him that resisted the despair I know he felt. We are young, he and I, just out of college and secure in our private world because of his money, our love, and our health. Sometimes I think we have been betrayed by our safe lifestyles, and have missed a time of easy, base, pure love, the period of our greatest freedom. Other times I feel like a bird that has just succeeded in its struggle to break from the white blindness of its shell and confronts for the first time the overwhelming red plumage of its father and the first shadows of night, and wants only to crawl back.

Tonight Martin and I go to the opera. We sit in our finery with all the gentlemen and ladies; I'm astonished at their beauty, at the opulence of the gilded theater. When the opera comes on I don't understand any of it—it's not my background as it is Martin's. But that's good because I can make of it what I wish—just as Martin anthropomorphizes his flowers in his journal, just as I try, and fail, to re-create the city with my pictures. In this way the cumbersome stage presences of the singers and their overwrought surroundings are overcome: I close my eyes and just listen. Hours, days, years later, we leave, and outside the theater the night sounds have gained their own music in my altered ears. We forgo a taxi to the Village, choosing to stroll through the Upper West Side. For a time, as we walk with arms linked, silent, the worlds of surreality and reality blur like the change of seasons, and it is easy to believe that it is still summer long after the cold has swept in.

Still far from home, we stop outside a flower shop and look through its rose-tinted windows. The flowers, some dried, some freshly cut, others still growing, lie heaped in naked abandon in vases, in baskets, strewn on the window shelf. "Aren't they beautiful?" is all I can think of to say, and I feel close at hand an understanding of why I love Martin. My reflection in the window reminds me of a time earlier tonight, when I'd said to Martin's image in the dressing room, "You love me because you've turned me into part of your world." In the mirror I saw Martin's hand twitch, and a long red streak of makeup glazed my cheek. He paused then, grabbed a rag, and scrubbed the mark from my face. "Sshh," he said, "you're going to make us late." Beside me now, he doesn't speak, but gazes with his rapturous child's eyes. I point to some and say, "What are those?" They are many-colored and full as an aroused nipple, made up of thousands of tiny protruding needle-like petals. "Those are poppies," he says, "flower of sleep, and dreams, and death. Of unreality." There is a sound behind us, and even as we turn I see the reflection of three men in the window, over the poppies, dulling their charm. Facing them, I see they are even dirtier than their reflection in the glass, and one carries in his hand a lead pipe, long and jagged at its end and devoid, in this light, of any color. "Money," they say, "faggots." On my arm, I feel Martin's hand vibrate wildly; with his other he reaches for his wallet slowly, pulls it out, hands it to them. They come in closer and push at us, pull us apart, steal from my wrist the gold watch Martin had given me, take its mate from him also. But as they reach to pull a ring from his finger Martin croaks hoarsely and lashes at one of the muggers. I turn to him and don't recognize his contorted face. He doesn't notice me as he strikes out again. I hear an unintelligible siren, then realize it's his voice, a scream of both fury and terror. His arms flail, his feet kick out blindly. I look to Martin's eyes, narrowed to slits, searching for something. I don't know what sign I'm looking for, but I know it's not there, and that terrifies me. All three are fighting him now, and I stand stunned, helpless, watching, thinking, This isn't real, this can't be happening. It's too crowded for the man with the pipe to use it, and Martin, in his rage, seems to be holding his own. But then the other two fall back, and the third steps in and raises his pipe. I see a hand as it strikes the window of the shop, hear seconds later the blaring alarm announcing the pain of glass splintering into the hand, and I feel the wind of the blurred arc of red as the hand flies. The wedge of glass slices through the neck of the man with the pipe, and then the glass drops to the ground, shattering into useless, diamond-bright fragments. The mugger stands there stupidly for a moment, pipe raised like an icon above his head, and then his neck belches blood all over Martin, himself, and me, staining our dark tuxedos red. I can't hear the pipe as it falls to the ground because of the alarm crying from the florist's shop, and then the man, his round mouth open like a startled child's, crumples in silence.

All I can hear, as though it were the illusory sea of a conch in my ear, is Martin's raspy breathing. All I see is him standing wilted, blind, and old inside his bloodstained suit. "Martin?" I stutter. He heaves a breath, screams at me, "Shut up, John, just shut up!" I look at him, don't know him: I have never known him. Inside the florist's window poppies, roses, and even other flowers lie scattered, the destroyed remnants of Martin's chain. Then, from a distance, there is a policeman's plain, loud, insistent voice, demanding, "Who's hurt, is anybody hurt? What happened here?"

CIRCUMNAVIGATION

I

Water was draining from Martin's bath, and threads of mist hung in the air. I'd just finished shaving. I was almost ready to help him from the tub when a long fart bubbled out of the water, filling the bathroom with sound and smell. Didn't know you still had it in you, I said without turning, and I washed the shaving cream off my face. Then I heard flesh slide in the tub, followed by a thump and the sound of splashing water. Quietly, Martin said my name. The word hung in the damp smelly air before falling on my shoulders, and something, some unexpected weight, made me study my face in the mirror before I responded to him, as if this would be the last time I'd ever see it. I suppose it looks the same now as it did then—my hair is still brown and straight and fine, my eyebrows are full, my eyes light blue, my nose is a little too big, my jawline's not as strong as it could be.

With an effort, I can harden the curves in my face, turn them into angles, give my face a definition. But left alone it's just round, a blob, and when I heard Martin try to stand again, and then fall again, when he said John again, more insistent but with less strength, everything went slack and my face fell apart. Behind me, water slapped the tub's sides, and when I turned, Martin was looking at it slosh between his legs. He didn't see my face, and I made an effort to pull it together. Martin's back was bowed, the notches of his vertebrae stood out like walnuts, his legs splayed like those of a baby who's just fallen, and the weight of his chin pressed on the catheter that poked from his chest. He was looking at a thick red and brown stream that leaked from his anus and ran between his legs down the center of the tub to the drain. Though it wavered some, it still went straight to the drain and disappeared. One of my hands reached out to Martin then, but the other, faster, found the doorknob behind me and turned it. Though our bathroom was small, it was not so small I could have one hand on the doorknob and touch Martin with the other, and I clung to the doorknob. Then Martin's head raised as if pulled by a puppeteer's string, his eyes rolled up and fastened themselves to mine, and his left hand jumped from its place on his leg like a white frog and landed on the edge of the tub. No, he said, and I realized that what my face looked like meant nothing to him, but still, I made the effort, I kept it tight.

The doorknob slipped through my sweaty fingers, and when the latch popped behind me, I knew that opening it was useless. I stepped forward then and bent down to Martin and gave him my right hand. He took it, squeezed it, under the skin his bones moved. *Just stay here,* he whispered, and then his hand went slack in mine and he rested his head on his chest again. Purple clots slipped out of him now, small turds rolled in the current. When nearly all the water was gone, I turned on the shower to keep the shit and blood from pooling in the bottom of the tub. The water fell on the back of Martin's head and on the tub, diluting but not obscuring the red and brown path carved against the white enamel as Martin's life slipped out the drain. Martin's hair was long then, the water's weight pulled it around his face in dark ragged lines. With the fingers of my free hand I combed it back, the water pulled it down again and I combed it back again, and as I did this I saw my face without aid of a mirror, felt it—hanging jaw and drooping eyelids, nose shapeless as a balloon—and I realized that I'd let go again, that even if Martin managed to raise his head and look at me, I couldn't save myself, not even to save him.

My mind wandered, through memories of a trip we'd taken to Miami Beach the previous year, *Six Days of Sex* we'd called it, though mostly we drowsed on the sand, and I remembered flying here, to Kansas, two years ago when we'd moved from New York, and Martin, just struck by crypto, spent the flight in the bathroom with diarrhea. I remembered we needed groceries, then I realized we didn't. Which is just to say that not even death commands your full attention. Not mine, and not Martin's: I kept saying *Shit* over and over again, the way, I suppose, the way that I wanted to say *No,* and I wasn't really *aware of it until Martin said, Actually, I think it's the blood loss that's going to do me in, and then he laughed at himself, just a couple of wet chuckles, but that's all that had passed for laughter from him for a while, and the way his shoulders shook and the way his bones poked at his wet skin made me think of old rice-paper lanterns shaking in the wind, starting to melt in the rain, and when his body moved, blood and shit spurted out of him in clouds.*

After a while the stream coming from Martin's body was just red, and then it was clear, and for a moment I thought the water draining from the tub came from his body, and then I realized, Of course, he's stopped hemorrhaging, and then, when I touched him with my left hand—my right hand can't really feel temperature—I noticed that his skin was no warmer than the water coming from the shower and that the water had gone cold long ago. And when his body folded over at the waist and the pressure forced another long, smelly fart out of him and his face smacked the tub's bottom, I didn't think it was like a rice-paper lantern being closed, I thought it was like the body of a six-foot-two-inch man who weighed eighty pounds and who'd had all the shit and blood and water and air sucked out of him folding over in death. I shut off the shower then and watched the last water drain out of the tub, pulling strands of Martin's hair with it, and I followed it down, through the pipes, into the cesspool, and then into the drum of a sewer-cleaning truck, and the truck drives to some fallow field and empties its fertile load of HIV-infected shit and blood, and the virus seeps down into the earth, into the aquifer, into every kernel of wheat and every grain of grass and every human and every animal that eats of the grain and grass, and I imagined all of them, every human, every animal, all dying, and I did not care. In Kansas, in New York and California and Canada and Mexico, in Europe and Asia and Africa and South America, all around the world, they could all die and I would not care.

My face felt swollen and shapeless, like a moldy orange, as though grief had been shoved into my mouth like a handful of seeds. It felt uncomfortable in my mouth, but I didn't know what to do, whether to spit, or just swallow.

THE GILDED

THEATER

I

I don't know jewels, I remember saying. I remember saying, To me, all green precious stones are emeralds. Jade, someone said. Oh yes, I nodded, jade. Tourmaline, said another voice. Tourmaline? I said. Tourmaline, tourmaline, other voices said, trying to roll over the vowels with the same ease the first voice had. I knew neither word nor stone; imagining, I saw an emerald or jade or nothing, just black letters. Then I saw a smiling face. I'll buy you one, it said. Oh no, I said, I don't even know you. Martin, he said, just as he'd said tourmaline, and that name, too, meant nothing to me. No, I said again, flustered, turning away. It seemed he followed me around the party for a while, but at some point I realized that I was following him, and when that happened I stepped in front of him as he'd stepped in front of me and I said, Tourmaline. Nothing moved in the room until he smiled. His teeth were perfect. Pearls, I said, and when he got it he laughed, and he leaned over then, and kissed me.

*　　*　　*

I met him the next day at a jewelry store. The hand Martin waved over the glass rack was impressive, palm large, fingers long and slender, nails buffed almost to a shine. A tan stretched from fingertips to underneath his cuff-linked arm; a wide coil of silver gleamed on his right ring finger. Tourmaline, he said, almost proudly, as if he already owned them. I leaned over the jewels that had been taken out of the case and mouthed a silent O. This piece of a word disturbed a few dust motes, which my eye followed down, ignoring the hundreds of green crystals resting on their black velvet bed, until another hand appeared, this one darker than Martin's, covered with black hair and three thick knots of gold. A voice asked, Which one you like, sir? I stood up, turned to Martin, who waited with his hands folded atop his belt buckle, grinning. I don't know, I said, they're too beautiful, too, too much—you decide. Martin's grin grew to a smile instantly. Too much for you? he said. Never! His hands suddenly swept the jewels into a single gleaming pile, and the man behind the counter smiled then, and folded his hands on his stomach exactly as Martin had. We'll take all of them, Martin told the man, who smiled a moment longer, then turned to fetch something large enough to contain the mass of jewels. Martin told me, You can choose later. For now, just know that they're yours for the asking. I nodded, but I was ignoring him. I was thinking of the man, and how quickly he'd come to imitate Martin.

*   *   *

My best friend's birthday is coming up, Martin said, soon after we met. I want you to come with me. But I don't even know him, I said. Her, Martin corrected me. Susan. You will love Susan, and Susan will love you. Besides, Martin said, it's *my* party. We had much to do, it seemed, but if there was a plan I never discerned it. We stopped in one store, purchased silver service for twenty. In another, Martin weaved his way in and out of hundreds of lamps, some on tables, some hanging by gilt chains, others growing from the floor, all of them turned on. The store seemed flooded, mostly by heat, and light. I felt seasick. That one, Martin pointed, and that one and that one and that one. When we shopped for Susan's party, I could never tell what were decorations and what were presents. A half hour in the light store proved too much for me, and I stepped outside for some air. A gust of wind swirled out with me, picked up a few leaves, set them down, and I sat on the curb. Martin was beside me in an instant. What's the matter? he demanded. Nothing, I said, it was just hot in there, the light hurt my eyes. Just a moment, Martin said; he put his head inside the door and called out an address. Send everything there, he said, and then he had an arm around me, hailed a taxi, pushed me in, felt my forehead for a temperature. Martin, I'm fine, I was just a little hot. In the taxi's dark interior, wind from open windows cooled the sweat on my skin. Martin's ministrations, like everything else about him, seemed overdone. Sure, Martin said, okay, fine, his voice quiet, subdued almost. He put his hands on his lap. I felt bad then, as if I'd spurned him, and I took his hand in mine, but then I let go of it. Did it burn you? Martin said. What? I said. Oh no, it's just . . . I took his hand and turned it palm up. A diamond, a huge diamond, was mounted on his silver ring. Oh, Martin said, and wagged his fingers. Light caught the diamond, and it winked at me. I thought it was a wart, I said. Martin laughed. No, he said, it was my father's. Why do you wear it like that? I asked. It's the only thing I'm afraid of having stolen, I guess. He shrugged then, and closed his hand. The diamond disappeared. My parents didn't leave us much, he said, except money.

In time, I came to understand Martin's apartment, but on that first visit I was lost. Perhaps I *was* feverish, I thought, perhaps delirious, perhaps I sleepwalked. A circular elevator took us to it, and when the doors opened we stood in the apartment's center, and then Martin strode away, and I waited in the elevator until I realized that I was one or two hundred feet above the ground and held in space only by a wire, and I stepped out of the elevator onto a floor made of yellow bricks, and the doors closed behind me. I looked around. My first impression was that the Sydney Opera House had cracked open and fallen on its side. The yellow bricks, I saw, weren't the whole floor, but only a four-foot-wide strip that disappeared into the apartment. Then Martin returned around a bend in a wall, his left sleeve rolled up to his elbow, a damp cloth draped over that forearm and a glass in his left hand. Aspirin, he said, and he dropped the pills into my mouth with his right hand and held the glass as I drank. I was still swallowing the aspirin's bitter taste when Martin began to swab my face with the cloth, and surprised at how good it felt, I closed my eyes against the cool water leaking off my forehead. The thing to remember, Martin said, leading me by the hand on a widening circle through his apartment, is that in Oz the yellow brick road always leads to the Emerald City. We stood at the door of an oval room with walls covered in softly glowing, lazily wandering tubes—blue, red, green, yellow, purple—whose path was interrupted only where they arched over doors or French windows. The room's dimensions were lost in color. The Emerald City? I asked. Aurora borealis actually, Martin said. I just shrugged, and walked to one of the windows. Looking down, I nearly fell over with dizziness, because we were so high that all I could see was blue sky, clouds, a plane flying far below us. Then I realized there was a balcony beyond the window and its mirrored floor reflected the sky. But when I stepped away from the view, my queasiness stayed with me, and I made my way to the only object I recognized in the room—the bed. Are you still hot? Martin asked, and I nodded. I unbuttoned my shirt, lay down. Martin adjusted a dial on the wall, and air surged from floor vents, and then slivers of green silk lifted up and began waving in the air, dancing like tendrils of seaweed on the ocean floor. And I'll say this much: I knew something was wrong, even then. With him, with me, with the combination? That I didn't know.

Morning at Martin's: it took me by surprise. I opened my eyes to a room that had just enough noise in it to seem unearthly quiet: the air from the vents, the rustle of the dancing fabric, the hum of the gas in the a.b. tubes, Martin's breathing beside me. It took me a second to place each of these sounds, and when I noticed the last I turned and put my arm around him and relaxed into the memory of the sex we'd had last night. That's when I noticed my shirtsleeve on my arm, and I could remember no sex, and I realized I must have fallen asleep as soon as I'd gone to bed. I rolled away from Martin then, feeling like I'd assumed an intimacy I hadn't earned, and this finally pulled me out of his strange bedroom, and I noticed myself then, my stomach and my head, both of which were spinning. You awake? I heard. Yes, I said quietly. Martin's body leaned over mine; in a few places, through my clothes, we touched. Would you like something? For my stomach, I said, not aspirin. I lay on my side and didn't look at him, though I felt his eyes on me. How about the bathroom? he said finally, and I let him lead me by the hand through a door into a room that looked more like a bathroom than the bedroom had looked like a bedroom: sink, tub, towels on the wall, things like that. He stood me next to something urn-like, filled with water. What's this? I said. The toilet. Right, I said, and threw up. Martin put a hand on my neck while I bent over, and when he rubbed back and forth his diamond scratched me lightly. After he flushed, I said, I should've never eaten that cheeseburger. I take it you're not Jewish, then, Martin said, leading me to the bedroom. Didn't my New Testament name give it away? I said, and I almost didn't hear us laughing, because I was thinking that Martin's wasn't the kind of joke I laughed at, and mine wasn't the kind of joke I told.

There is something languorous, indulgent even, about making love in the afternoon, when you're just a little ill. You have to do absolutely nothing. Even kiss him back and he'll be rewarded, and he'll stroke your body all the more passionately, and he'll keep asking you things like How do you feel? (good) Am I hurting you? (no) Do you want me to stop? (no, no), and if, when it's over, you turn from him without a word to fall asleep, he will feel like he's done his job well, and he'll put an arm around you, and he'll say, I'm just going to be quiet now, so you can fall asleep, and then he'll keep talking, saying nothing, saying, I'll fix us a light supper later that won't upset your stomach, saying, Mmmm, and wetting the back of your neck with his tongue until you do fall asleep, feeling like you're pressed up against the stomach of a mother cat, who licks you until you're wet, and then until you're dry, and clean.

*　　*　　*

There are many ways he could've kept me. The easiest
would have been leaving me in his apartment and not showing me how to get out. But instead, somehow, he did this
to my heart. I feel like claiming that he pulled it from my
chest and locked it in a cage. But if he did, then it was a
cage so finely wrought—or should I just call it opulent?—
that even after I became aware of it, I was so fascinated
by its design I didn't notice that, in his own way, Martin
limited my experience far more than it had been before I
knew him. But this knowledge came later; that weekend,
only Monday came, and I said, I need to go to work. You're
sure you feel okay? is all he said. I nodded. We'd better get
you something to wear. He pointed to my clothes on the
floor. Those are unsuitable for human habitation. Where
do you work? At the *Journal of the American Medical As-
sociation*. I copy-edit. Martin made a face and flipped a
switch beyond a door, producing enough light to overwhelm
the a.b. tubes surrounding it. Nothing too flashy, then, he
said, and disappeared. He came back a moment later with a
severe-looking black suit and a white shirt with a large red
rose sewn on the left front panel. But it was the silk briefs
that made me pause. Martin, my clothes are fine, really.
Nonsense, Martin said, I'll have them cleaned, they'll be
ready tonight. I sat on the bed, damp from my shower, still
naked, holding the boxers in my lap. I'm not sure I'm free
to come by tonight. Work keeps me really busy during the
week. Martin threw a pair of socks at me. Then I'll have

them sent to your place. What's your address? I looked at him. From somewhere, pen and paper had materialized in his hands, and he sat on a chair I hadn't seen before. I laughed then, just a little—this place was too much. And then, when I realized I didn't want him to have my address, I stopped. I have to bring your clothes back to you, I said. Martin looked up from his pad, his face bright. Then I'll see you tonight? Wonderful!

People commented on the suit. Seth, the other fag in the office, said, That's an Armani. I know Armani. How did *you* afford *Armani* on *your* salary? I debated whether to tell him, finally decided that the story was already too strange, and besides, I'd rather be mysterious. One thing I didn't consider, however, was the idea that Martin and I might not go on seeing each other—that we might not be worth talking about. I believed that gifts from him, unlike those from other lovers, were no real indication of interest—later I'd realize I'd been wrong—but still, there'd been something definite about the eager way he'd looked at me that morning and the hungry kiss he'd given me at the elevator. We're not supposed to take personal calls at work, I'd told him, I'll call you. You do that, he said. That enigmatic smile, and the door closed. I was at my desk, caught in a passage about the relationship of green leafy vegetables and coronary occlusion, when I remembered that the funny thing was, he'd never asked for my number.

*   *   *

Perhaps it was her name, but I'd pictured her as a Susan Sontag type, and she did resemble a young version of her. The same thick black hair which was always almost messy, the same strong shoulders, a tendency to be photographed in dark clothes. The first thing she said to me was, Don't let him get to you. Martin had been right: I liked her immediately. What do you mean? I asked, following her into her kitchen, where it was less noisy. Already I'd been comforted by the large rectangular rooms of her apartment. Susan opened the fridge, took out a carton of orange juice, poured it into a glass pitcher. She said, He has too much money but no imagination, so he finds other people to do the thinking for him. She paused for a moment. I wonder what he's doing with you, then. What do you mean? I asked. John, she said, the reason why I've always liked Martin is that he's interested in people as personalities, not acquisitions. Susan—I began, but she put up her hand. Now, now, she said, I realize I'm not giving you the benefit of the doubt. She used her hip to push open the kitchen door, and smiled at me as the noise from her party rushed in from the living room. When I figure out what it is he likes about you, you'll be the first to know. Now wish me a happy birthday and let's be festive. Happy birthday, I said to her back; already she was yelling over the din. Martin, she called, there's a performance at the Nuyorican you *must* see. But if Martin heard her he didn't respond. He was dancing in the living room, surrounded by the lamps he'd bought—I still wasn't sure if they were gifts or decoration. All at once he began to spin in a circle, and a cape he'd tied around his neck earlier began to float away from his body. The other dancers fell back, laughing. Martin spun and spun. How long could he keep it up, I wondered. The cape, held aloft by his arms and the force of his spin, unfurled around him in a full circle so that he seemed like a child's kaleidoscopic top, the black silk of his cape catching the many lights and separating them into reds and blues, greens, violent purples; on the wooden floor his shiny slippers did the same, only the light hit them less frequently, flashing as though off jewels or water. He'll trip, I thought, he'll grow dizzy and fall. He looked like a vampire of the Bram Stoker variety, except for his perfect tan. He looked nuts. How long can he keep it up? I thought. But I never found out—I turned away first, in some way overwhelmed, and there was Susan, smiling, combining two half-full bowls of pretzels, saying, Now, what did I say? Don't let him get to you.

You need a look, Martin said one morning after breakfast. At what? I asked. No, you need to look *like* something. How about an armadillo? I've always wanted to look like an armadillo. Martin left me on the couch, walked across what I called the *Challenger* lounge: uncomfortable, space-age plastic furniture, recessed TVs, a fireburst print on the wall. You're being defensive, he said. I hugged the couch's arm to keep from slipping into the empty space where Martin had sat and waited for the cushion to reinflate. I thought defensiveness was expected of a person who's been told he looks inadequate, I said, and crossed my legs. I had to catch myself then with both hands to keep from sliding off the couch's narrow seat. I didn't say you looked inadequate—it's just that you look like every other gay boy in off the farm from Kansas. Two things, I said, uncrossing my legs and regaining my balance. First, I'm more likely to meet two guys from the same alpine village at one of your parties than another gay boy from Kansas. It's one of my selling points. Martin folded his arms across his chest and smiled. The second thing? he asked. The second thing is that I wasn't raised on a farm. I grew up in a city of two hundred thousand people. My apologies, Martin said. Now, would you like to see what I have in mind? Perhaps something in latex, I suggested. Martin looked at me seriously. Latex? Why? Well, I said, pushing myself up again, I'm sure the adhesiveness would keep me from slipping off this damn couch! Martin laughed. You have a sense of humor, I love that. But seriously, he said, and pulled something from a drawer. This is more of what I had in mind. He walked over and handed me a framed photograph. His diamond, exposed to the light, distracted me for a moment, and then, when I looked at the picture, I didn't know if I should be more shocked by its subject or by its autograph. To M, it said, after Key West. Martin, I said, this is James Dean. I don't look anything like James Dean. Precisely, Martin said. Precisely.

That evening, my apartment: as I let myself in the door,

arms burdened with packages, I realized that this was the first time I'd seen its three rooms, counting bathroom, in a week. I dropped the packages on the floor, sat on the futon. Across the room, I saw my reflection in a window: my new hair, lightened, was piled on top of my head. I ran my fingers through it until it flattened. My fashion make-over, Martin had called it, but it—and all these packages—seemed like much more than that. A gust of wind shook the window, and I got up and opened it. Outside, below, trash was swirling over the sidewalk, and I let the wind mess up my hair even more. While I stood there the buzzer rang. Florist, said an anonymous voice, male, tough, when I answered the second buzz. A few minutes later an enormous vase of roses sat atop the TV, the only surface in my apartment large enough to hold them. There were so many that the light of a floor lamp beside the TV changed color as it passed through them and cast a pink shadow on the floor. For just a second I was swept away by their beauty, and then I thought, He has my address, and a vague feeling of unease crept along my neck like a fur-legged spider. I lay back on the futon and looked at the flowers, listened to the wind blow. After a minute I shifted my gaze to the ceiling. There was something nice about it, I thought, all plain and white and bare. Nothing about it reminded me of Martin. Or of myself.

The next week we went to three gallery openings, one closing, two parties not related to art, and we dined out with Susan at least three times. One meal stands out. I remember it only because I'd asked Susan—in jest, I'd thought—if she'd figured out why Martin liked me. He was in the bathroom. No, she said, and pulled at a strand of her hair. But I will tell you this. She seemed serious, and I remember leaning forward in my chair. There are three mistakes I've seen men make with Martin: They tell him they love him. They don't tell him they love him. She paused, and looked behind me. Turning, I saw Martin approaching. And the third? I prompted, facing her again. The third thing is, they begin to expect money from him, and they take it without asking. Well, I said, I'm in no danger of doing that. Months later, at another meal, Susan would tell me that I was the first person she'd ever seen leave Martin with his desire unfulfilled. What about *my* desire? I would ask. Susan smiled, and I think she intended for that smile to resemble Martin's. What about it? she asked. And, now that I think about it, something else happened at that first meal. We'd been talking about death—not death exactly, but ways of dying. I don't remember much of what we said, but I do remember that at one point Martin turned on me after I said something. His smile was missing and his face, and voice, seemed cold without it. He said, I will certainly not die of something as ordinary as AIDS, John. How—he paused, searching for a word—how *mundane*!

I was in the lounge with the comfortable chairs when I heard Martin's voice. John, it said, and then it laughed. I looked up guiltily. I'd been watching myself in a mirror, studying the way I draped one black-dungareed leg over the other, the way I slouched in a chair so that my chest—a chest James Dean never had—was shown to its best advantage. A large tourmaline, just back from the jeweler, hung on a silver chain from my neck. John, I heard again, and then rustling water. Martin, I called, where are you? John, John, John, came Martin's voice, holding each word out, and then another laugh. I'm in the john, John. Martin—I started, but his voice cut me off. Follow the yellow brick road, Martin sang, and I confess, after four weeks of his apartment I still used it to help me find my way to the bedroom, which was empty. Then I saw a light in the bathroom. Martin, back to me, naked, stood in a tub of water singing into the intercom. Follow the, follow the, follow the, follow the— Martin, I said. He turned jerkily, as if he stood in mud, not water. John, he said. He scooped up a double handful of water. Love-ly, he said, breaking the word in half, and then nothing more. I walked to him. His body was beautiful even without clothes. It betrayed no hint of his age. Only his penis was wrinkled, but then, I suppose, every man's is. I thought he was offering me cupped hands full of water, and I leaned forward. It looked clean. It even sparkled, as though his hands held not one but a thousand diamonds. He's bathing in Per- rier, I thought, perhaps even champagne, and I smiled. Maybe he saw the reflection in his hands, but just as my tongue touched the liquid's surface and I tasted a hardness,

Martin opened his hands and a hundred crystals and a little water spilled to the floor, clattering. Martin pulled me into the tub suddenly, and even as I yelled, Martin! My pants! my legs drove through what felt like warm ice, and then Martin was pulling me to him and kissing me and pushing down my pants, the crystals and water in the tub rumbling like thunder, the tourmaline a lump between our chests, and Martin's hands, like his voice had been, were everywhere. The last thing I saw before closing my eyes was the dye of my new pants leaching into the water and surrounding each crystal, and I thought the tub looked like it was full of oil and water, and I thought I could drop a match into it and it would burst into flame. And all I could think was that no one—*no one*—would ever hold me like that again.

Martin's hair: it's what first comes to mind when I think of the night we took the subway. I remember its thick luxuriance, and I remember how I rested my hand under his occipital bone while we watched a Nuyorican performance, and I remember rubbing my fingers against the crewed back and pushing them into the longer hair on top of his head. I remember how his hair waved in the heavy wind that blew on us as we walked the unnumbered streets of the Lower East Side, looking for a subway station. He'd insisted we take a train and ignored my request to get a cab. His head was the only part of his body, besides his shoes, visible under his ash-colored plastic Miyake trench coat, which inflated in the wind and made Martin seem, from the back, like a bloated Michelin man. When we finally found a station Martin was so unused to taking the subway that he steered us to the downtown line and we were well on our way to Brooklyn before he realized our error. He got up and studied a subway map for a moment, then came back to me and announced that we could switch to the uptown line at Boro Hall. I just nodded my head. Then there was a long silence between us, only train sounds, and I fell asleep. Martin woke me at Boro Hall, and holding hands, we ascended one flight of stairs and descended another, and we sat down on a bench in the deserted station. I fell asleep again, and was awakened this time by voices. How you doing, honey? I opened my eyes to see a pale arm littered with freckles and long black hairs interpose itself between my head and Martin's. That's some sharp clothes you and your girlfriend have on. Where'd you get them? Martin's voice, behind the arm, said, A friend made them for me. A friend, huh? I leaned forward to look at the body connected to the arm and the voice: it was a young white boy, not more than eighteen, with a thick build and a couple of zits on his forehead. That's some friend, he was saying, and he squeezed Martin's shoulders visibly and shook him a little. Martin's hand tightened around mine. Maybe I ought to get his number from you, give him a call. That's some nice suit. Martin smiled and said, He works out of Paris. Paris! the boy said loudly. Shit, boys, I don't think my ma would let me call Paris. For a moment I thought "boys" referred to Martin and me, but then I heard chuckles and I looked up. Five other boys, about the same age as this one, were standing around. One of them, a black boy whose baggy shirt and pants concealed the shape of his body, said, Johnson, you don't do nothing else your mother says to, and I don't see you starting now. All of the boys laughed, and Martin laughed with them. Trying not to move my lips, I said, Let's go, Martin. No one said anything for a moment, and Martin tightened his squeeze on my hand. The diamond now poked at the skin between two of my fingers. Suddenly Martin said, So you're Johnson? This is my lover, John. I'm Martin. Something happened then: the three names floated from Martin's mouth like smoke and dispersed in the dank air of the subway terminal, until they lost meaning, and all at once I realized I knew as little about Martin—and about myself—as I did about this Johnson, and that's when my fear shifted from him to Martin. You're lovely, huh? Johnson was saying. One of the other boys said, Hey, lovely, you like it like this? and spun one of his friends around and shot his pelvis against the other's buttocks. Everyone laughed, including Martin, who laughed easily, and that's when I had to close my eyes. I concentrated on my hand. Even though I could feel Martin's diamond clearly, could tell that it was cutting into the web between two of the fingers of my left hand, I couldn't tell which two. Behind my closed eyes, I heard Martin and the boys, talking, laughing. Occasionally, at a really loud laugh, I opened my eyes to see one of the boys pretending to butt-fuck another. Martin's grip on my hand grew tighter and tighter, his laughter louder and louder, and I shut my eyes so hard that colors—like the a.b. tubes' —moved behind my lids. Eventually a rhythm established itself behind the laughter and the half-heard words, a tapping that grew slowly louder until it had the clear sound of wood on flesh, and everyone stopped laughing. I looked up and saw a cop. He smacked his hand with his billy club. Why don't you get the hell out of here? He was talking to us. To Martin and me, I mean. To Martin and John.

We took a cab. He was silent through Brooklyn's unfamiliar streets, silent on the bridge, silent all the way through Manhattan, as one neighborhood after another yielded to the cab's forward motion, until we were on our street, and still it was unfamiliar. Upstairs, in Oz, Martin strobed the a.b. tubes and fixed me with his smile. The lights did terrible things to his teeth. God, that was fun, he said, stripping off his trench coat. Light flashed through a small hole in its side, and I don't know how but I *knew* what had happened. I grabbed the coat, put my finger through the hole. What's this, Martin? I demanded. He shrugged his shoulders. Nothing. I went to the place on his body where the hole would be if he were wearing the coat. There was another hole there, in his jacket. And this, Martin, I said, pulling the jacket off him and poking my finger through the second hole. What's this? Nothing. Nothing, I repeated. And I suppose this is nothing too? I said, and I went to jab my finger through the red-tinged hole in his white shirt, but then I stopped. No, Martin, I said, pointing, that's something. Martin just shrugged off the shirt, and I saw the scraped part of his skin where a knife, Johnson's knife, had cut, and I saw dried blood on his skin. John, Martin said. His smile. I feel so horny right now. Martin— I started, but he grabbed me and closed my mouth with his. I pushed away from him as though he were mugging me. What did he *do* to you? I asked. Then Martin leaped at me with his index fingers extended. He poked them into me at various places on my body: my stomach, my chest, my face, my arms when I moved them to cover my face. Stop! I screamed, but he kept jabbing me until I pushed him so hard he fell on the bed. We looked at each other for a long time without speaking, and then a grin split Martin's face and he ran to a window, slid it open, stepped onto the balcony, and let out a whoop of pure pleasure and exhilaration. Wind blew into the room, carrying leaves and a few pieces of paper, smashing flat the lines of silk that danced over the floor vents. I followed Martin to the balcony. I remember that I tried to understand. I pulled at my hair the way they do in movies, as if I could pull understanding right out of my brain, and that's when Martin, the lights of the city and the a.b. tubes reflecting off his face, that's when he turned to me and said, John, stop messing up your hair, you're always messing up your hair. I looked at him, I can imagine how stupidly. What? I said. The whole idea is for it to stand up, Martin said, the way James's used to, and the more you run your fingers through it, the flatter it gets. Confused, I started to run my fingers through it again, but I caught myself. I stared at my hands, and then I shoved them in my pockets. I wanted to say something, but I didn't know what. I said, I don't understand, Martin. Martin said, That's what Susan was supposed to tell you. I just looked at him. I was beyond asking. His hair moved in the wind, and I could feel my hair on my head, imitating his. What I like about you, he said. She was supposed to tell you what I like about you, wasn't she? It's that you don't understand.

And he was right. I didn't, and I would never. I turned from him then, walked to the edge of the balcony, looked up the broad avenue. The wind rushed down it, gathering speed—and debris as well, as it scooped up everything that lay on the street and sidewalks, and the raindrops that had begun to fall seemed thrown. I turned away from the city and looked at my feet. There was that disorienting mirrored floor: my feet seemed unnaturally large, my body impossibly long, my head lost in the night clouds, and, at such a distance, almost unrecognizable as me. I closed my eyes and heard the click-click of Martin's shoes on the glass as he approached me; when I opened them I saw in the mirror his legs right behind mine. Black shoes, black pants: it seemed like a shadow had been grafted to my body, and when I saw a blurred arc as his hand reached out to touch me, I turned suddenly and said, No! I looked at his smiling face, tinged now by a hint of confusion, a touch of foul humor. Was this also part of my shadow? The wind at my back pushed me toward him, and Martin crossed his arms and waited, as if my approach were inevitable. But when it seemed I could hold out no longer and would fall into him, I rushed past him and jumped, and I felt the wind rush up my pant legs and loose my shirt from my belt, spinning me wildly and carrying me far, far away from him. When I came down finally I was alone. A few other things tumbled from the sky with me: a mauve felt hat with the eye of a peacock feather tucked in the band, a plastic watch, and many, many pieces of paper, some of them dollar bills. I ignored them all, started walking. I didn't understand what had just happened. I didn't try to. There are only a few variables, after all: earth, air, fire, water; birth, love, hate, death; above all, desire. Their combinations are infinite, but still, I've always tried to keep each element clear and discrete in my mind (mundane, Martin would say, ordinary) because when they run together they make something incomprehensible, uncontrollable, something—something opulent. And, like most people, I don't know what to make of opulence. Before Martin, I could only stare in awe. Now, I only ask its price.

LEE

∎

There's a layer of space between us, like a blanket. He doesn't know I've put it there, but I feel him note its presence, take advantage of the protection it offers. I say, Let me show you a trick, and I unroll a condom on his cock with my mouth. We laugh, neither of us says anything, and then I say, "I want it to feel like rape." He couldn't possibly understand why I ask him to do these things, but he does them anyway, for his own reasons, which are probably as simple as my own but which are as distant from my understanding as my reasoning is from his. This is the state of things between us when I scream for the first time. "Harder!" I yell into the blank pate of my bedroom: these blank walls, so recently emptied, like the inside of a hairless skull. "Fuck me harder!" I scream again, and he does. He's older, forty-five, maybe fifty, and his torso where it rises up and splits from mine is hairy, gray, sweaty in the dim light. His body rocks back, then smacks into mine again and again, and with each push I feel a twinge of pain as his penis tries to straighten a bend in my intestine. I want

*that twinge to grow into a stab. I scream again, beg him,
"Fuck me till I—" I cut myself off. I was going to say, Fuck
me till I bleed. This is my first mistake of the night, as for a
few moments I'm taken over by thoughts which tell me why
this man can't make me bleed.* Lying on my back, legs vertical
across his chest, feet in the air: he pushed at me but I couldn't
relax. Grunts of other men more successful at their endeavors
than we penetrated the thin door. With a sigh he said, Maybe
some other time, and I nodded. Then he bent one of my
legs forward and began massaging my toes, my instep, my
arch, the ball of my foot. Or maybe we should start at the
bottom, he said, and he said also, Don't worry, and he smiled.
I nodded again, exhausted, closed my eyes, chewed my lip.
With a crunch he bit my toe fiercely, my own teeth punctured
my lip, and then, when he loosened his jaws, I breathed out
all the air in my lungs. Every muscle of my body, which had
tensed toward my toe, relaxed for just a moment, and with
a push and a loud grunt he shoved his penis inside me. *Then
there's the room again, its barren walls, a piece of furniture
creeps into my line of sight: the dresser, its brown top swept
bare. I hear hard breathing. I look at him. His eyes are closed
and he's working his hips, he's smiling and biting his lip in
exertion. "Hit me!" I scream. His eyes pop open in fear, his
head snaps back, he stops fucking. I sit up on my elbows and
put my face right in his and yell, "Hit me! Smack my face!"
and I think the first time he strikes me just to push me away.
He waits a moment after the blow, lets the sound fade from*

*the room, and then he hits me on the other side of my face
and I feel the red heat of his hand sweep over the skin of my
cheek. He slaps me again, right hand, left hand, right hand,
left hand, and I squirm my ass around on his cock and moan
encouragement at him. He chuckles and mumbles something
under his breath, then starts to slide in and out of me again.
He stops for a second to hit me really hard, twice, and then
he grabs my ankles and begins fucking in earnest, grunting
with each push forward, sighing with each pull back. I'm dizzy
from those last two punches, my eyes are unfocused but point
toward the ceiling. My thoughts are confused too, they roll
through my head like water and slosh painlessly off the sides
of my skull.* His fingers were as thin as the cigarette he held
with them. He said, I wonder if you hate me as much as I
hate you. I said nothing, brought the pan of eggs to the table
and divided them between our plates. Deliberately, he flicked
ashes on his. He said, You only stay because I'm sick. Because
I'm helpless. Stop, I said, please. But he didn't stop: with
one finger he pushed his plate slowly toward the edge of the
table. Before it fell I grabbed it, moved it out of his reach,
and then I got up, went to him, sat on his lap. Ow! he cried.
Goddammit, get off me! His cigarette fell to the floor. As I
watched, the linoleum peeled back from the burning end
and turned black. I love you, I said. I wanted to scream.
*Things start to make sense. The ceiling, a long thin crack
stretching along its surface, comes sharply into focus. Emo-
tions seize me like a wild animal attacking from behind, claws*

dig into my shoulders and rake down my back, and I want to scream mindlessly, Will nothing make you go away? I kissed him. He pulled his head back and turned away, but he was crying. I love you, I said again, and then I left the room. And then, for just a moment, life gives me a brief, if maudlin, respite, as the lyrics to an old song, Feelings, wo wo wo feelings, float up to me like echoes in a deep well. He sang to me: he was drunk and he was dying and we were both laughing, and despite myself I laugh again. Above me, still fucking steadily, the man looks down at my laugh, smiles, laughs a little himself, and I sit up then and put my face right in his. "Stop," I hiss, and the man stops. And then he says that thing that every top says, even the ones that pay you: "Am I hurting you?" "A little," I tell him, though it's an answer he'll never understand, and then I'm silent long enough for his face to chill a little with fear. Fear, I wonder, that I'll ask him to leave, or fear that I'll ask him to violate me in yet another way? "Go to the closet," I say then, and he does, pulling out of me slowly so the condom doesn't come off and padding gingerly across the floor. The windows are open, I imagine the air must be cold on his bare feet. I want to feel sorry for him, but I also don't want to feel anything at all. The man stops at the closet door, doesn't open it until I tell him to. "Tell me what you see." He skips the obvious, the boxes on the shelf, the clothes on hangers, the shoes on the floor. "The gun?" he says. That question in his voice. I don't ask him to clarify. I lie back, look at the crack in the ceiling again. He cleaned the pus crusted around his catheter where it poked from his chest. He looked up and saw me in the mirror. Come here, he said. I walked to him. Stand behind me, he said. He pulled me so close that my chest pressed against his back and his hair tickled my nose. Then he bent his head to the side and I saw my head in the mirror perched above his body and I knew what he was doing, but I stood there and let him do it. Look carefully, he said, and I looked at his drooping nipples and the lines of his ribs and his ashen skin and my face. This is going to be you one day, he said. And I hope it's soon. *I pull out an old voice, my fuck-me-I'm-only-a-child voice, and I say, "It's always been my fantasy to get fucked by a gun." I want something to happen then, for a wind that isn't blowing to flutter a candle that isn't burning and send shadows that don't exist scurrying over the walls. But there's only a brief silence, and then the man says, "You want me to fuck you with the gun?" and, not trusting language, I sit up and look at him and nod my head. What I see is that his penis is softening, the condom wrinkled like sagging panty hose, gray and ugly in this light. What I see is the man reach in and grab my .22, take it from the closet, close the door behind him. What I think is, A younger man wouldn't do this, and then there's a blank spot of time and when things return I'm holding my knees with my hands and I feel an inch or two of cold steel sliding into my rectum and I imagine the long black barrel of the gun poking out of me like a dark extension of my spine. Questions should be asked: why do I want him to do this? and, now that he's actually started: why is he doing it? But I don't want to ask, I just want to replace one pain with another, or with nothing. A length of hollow steel starts working back and forth inside me, ramming me now, and again, and again, making me grunt with pain, making me hiss, making my mind a blank wall, bare of everything. And then, even then, it starts to adjust, my mind, I start to think again,* She was old and dry, her hair graying, her eyes hidden in wrinkles and she was only twenty-eight years old. The look they gave me was so overwhelmingly weak that I had to cover them with my hand, my hand with its crooked fingers and arthritic pains, my broken hand covered up those eyes which looked at me, which accused me, which told me more plainly than words, You are his son. Bruises old and new covered her arms, legs, back, breasts, face, and the jagged ends of broken bones made strange bulges under her skin. Light came down from the basement door at the top of the stairs and then it was gone, and there was just my father's shadow. *The gun is pounding into me deeper, but that's not why I'm moaning. I think, Not him, not her, not here, not now. I try to get control. I try to think about the gun. I make myself imagine that my asshole is an eye and I'm looking down the long tunnel of the gun barrel. It's dark, and at the other end I imagine I see a nick of light glint off the copper head of the bullet in the chamber, a little flash of death as the bullet takes off and starts its hundredth-of-a-second hurtle toward my body, where it will tear up each vertebra, destroy my spinal cord, leave behind an empty tube and an empty body, leave behind nothing but numbness. And then quietly, so quietly, I whisper, "Pull the trigger." "What?" the man whispers back, and though I want to I can't sit up, the gun is in me all the way up to my neck and I can only stare at the cracked ceiling and scream, "Pull the trigger!" The gun goes loose then as the man lets go of it without pulling it out of me. I sit up, see him backing away from the bed, and then it happens: the condom that had covered his penis and protected him from me slips off his limp dick and falls to the floor, and the splat it makes is loud, impossibly loud, in the silence of the room. The man reaches down and covers himself with his hands. He looks around until he sees his clothes, and then he dives for them, bundles them to his groin, runs out of the room. And I lie on my bed while he dresses in the other room, a rifle hanging from my anus like the shit-filled entrail of a slaughtered hog, and I cry quietly, and when the outside door opens, the pressure changes in the house and wind rushes in through the open windows of my room, the curtains fly from the windows like startled ghosts, but when the door closes, everything goes still again, as if the house has just been dropped behind a giant boulder. In the sudden quiet I hear myself sob aloud and I think that at last I've succeeded, for I cry only for myself, and if any thought of Martin remains, or of my mother, or of my father, they founder in a sea of other names, and nameless faces, and in the faces of hundreds of men whom I remember by a common name, a name that remains unconnected to any identity no matter how many times it is assumed. And that name, I must remind myself, is my own: John.*

F U C K I N G   M A R T I N

∎

I hate the empty moment before emotion clarifies itself. I hate sitting on Susan's couch and staring at her living room, which feels unfamiliar, even though nothing about it has changed. When she comes from the kitchen, carrying a platter of crackers that ring a smooth brown mound, she says, "Hummus," and dips a finger into the speckled-green paste. "I think they put parsley in it or something." Hummus. Parsley. The world revolves around this opposition for a moment, and then, when I've accepted it, I realize that I'm afraid. Susan sits on the couch, looks at me. I can see the curve of her breast through a gap between two open buttons of her shirt. It rises and falls with her breathing. I notice the dimmed lights, the hush, the new sound of wordless music, and into this heady air I breathe my first words of the night. "Susan," I say, "you have to risk AIDS in order to get pregnant." I wonder then, as her hands rush to her chest, if she undid the buttons deliberately.

*   *   *

Seduction was Martin's art. Sometimes on a Sunday morning, the light in the tiny rooms of our apartment softened by closed curtains, he told me old stories. In the living room, sprawled on a futon, or in the kitchen, as he fried bacon or made omelettes and I sat at the table. How loosely I held him in that small space, one hand around my coffee, the other tracing the waistband of his underwear, the smell of both—coffee, underwear—mixing in my nose. For a while the only sound would be his metal spatula scraping the pan, but when he started speaking it was like a catalogue, a litany, was unrolling from his mind. Martin had a great memory for names, places, dates, for technique, though soon I realized he wasn't bragging, or trying to make me jealous, or being sentimental. He wasn't trying to recapture his past—merely to validate its existence. The remains of those mornings are mental pictures that I've drawn from his words: Martin, in the Ramble, lowering his glasses, slowly undoing the buttons of his shirt. I remember how carefully he chose his words, as carefully as, in days past, he must have chosen his method. He didn't unbutton his shirt: he undid the buttons one by one, his fingers working down his chest, a V of skin spreading behind his passing hand like the wake of a boat. And he knew me too, knew that my own backward-looking eyes would revel in this knowledge of his past, that my mind would take it in like liquor, until the whole of his experience would become inseparable from my own, and it would seem that the words which had been mouthed in his ears had been whispered to me, and the hands which had run across his body had passed over mine. I don't remember, I *am* Martin: in a club, sliding a beer down the nearly empty gutter of a bar, coins tinkling to the floor as the bottle passes; in an alley, standing in shadow, listening to approaching footsteps, striking a match at just the right time. Though I'm sure he told me about the men he picked up, I don't remember their looks, why they attracted him, even if his seductions were successful. I did realize, even then, that he presented himself as an object, played roles out of movies and books; but he knew this too. You could in those days, John, he said. This was strange to me—not that he knew about roles, but that he had ever assumed them. I had played the pursuer in our relationship, had, on seeing him at Susan's old piano at one of her parties, pulled a rose from a jade vase and placed the half-open flower in his lapel buttonhole as he sat at the piano. I wonder, though: if I had possessed the ability to see him differently, would his piano playing have seemed a pose, a façade even more romantic than the one I'd assumed? But knowing that would require a different set of eyes, now, and in the past as well, and all I really know is what I remember: Martin—my lover Martin, the object Martin—posing himself for sex, for it is only that object which I now possess.

Memories pollute a planned atmosphere of seduction. Susan's apartment, if pared down to uneven wooden floors, cracked walls, and paint-smothered moldings, could be the one I once shared with Martin. I try to focus on her, but she pulls aside her hair and, beyond her shoulder, the ancient piano falls into view. Nostalgia traps us—the food, the music, everything, chosen according to past times. "My friend who likes hummus," Susan has called me—what about that is sexy? She speaks now in a careful voice. "Do you remember—?" she starts. She stops when she sees what I look at. She knows that I—that we both—remember. It seems all we can do, and that is why she doesn't finish her sentence. When Susan suddenly closes the windows, I think at first that she does so to foster the nostalgia, but when she sits down again there is more space between us than before. We both look at the new space, but neither of us moves into it.

I've been with a girl before—once, when I was eighteen, a long time ago. She and I had just finished our first year in separate colleges and were home for the summer. We'd known each other for years, had even been close friends in high school, but it took nine months apart and, that summer, the absence of most of our friends to force us together. Still, I think it's safe to claim we were experimenting, though not with sex; neither of us knew it about the other, but neither of us was a virgin. We were experimenting with love, and we failed. And it's not that I *didn't* love her, nor she me. Who knows, without love it might have been easier—certainly less painful.

We drove to the river one night in my father's old pickup.

It was late June, early July. Already there was something between us: movies in the evenings after work, weekends in stores trying on expensive clothes that we never bought, long good nights on her front porch that left me alone in bed with a hard-on. We did a lot of things, I realize, that created their own conversations or made words unnecessary. We never talked about ourselves. On the way to the river, I sped down rutted dirt roads and the cab was filled with engine noises and music that screeched out of the single-speaker AM radio. We sang along and laughed and cursed at the more vicious bumps. At the river we rolled our socks into our shoes and waded into the shallow, slick-like-oil water. We held hands. It was night, the sky clear, and I invest the stars now with great significance, because you don't really see them in the city and they have for so long been a symbol of romantic love. Ten feet away from the water the air had been hot and still, but in it we were cool, and laughed quietly at little jokes and skittered on stones hidden in the sand. Though we hadn't talked about it, we both knew what was going to happen.

It was on a sandbar, surrounded by water, that we spread an old holey blanket through which the sand penetrated so easily that soon she suggested we abandon it and stretch out directly on the ground. I said no, the ground was damp, and besides, it wasn't really ground, but sand, it would get all over us. A stupid argument followed—we didn't fight, but we became paralyzed by an inability to agree and eventually we fell silent, I half on, she half off the blanket. I remember lying there looking up at the stars and feeling the effort of not speaking growing harder and harder, when suddenly her face interrupted my view and she kissed me. The kiss went on for a long time, and then extended itself, as the rest of our bodies became part of it and our clothes came off. Then all at once she rolled off me, and even as I noticed that the blanket had become a wadded mass between us she said, John, do you remember Hank? and after I'd said yes, she said, I had a baby last April. His.

All at once things expanded: my mouth, my eyes, my mind, my arms and legs even, flung wide in an effort to catch the sky that seemed to be falling on me. Only one part of me shrunk. It's unfair to say that her sudden revelation did us in; really, she merely provided the excuse I'd been looking for. What she said didn't repel me, but just then— when I was wondering if I should put on a condom, wondering if this would feel as good as, or better or worse than, it did with boys—just then she made sex seem unerotic, less like fantasy, more like life.

She started to talk then; she told me about hiding in her dorm room because when she left it for meals or classes people pointed at her. Her friends advised her to abort. That was okay for other women, she said, but not for her. Counselors, her parents, people calling themselves her friends, told her to drop out and raise the baby; if possible, marry the father. That, too, was okay for other women, but not for her. She had plans, and besides, who knew where he'd run away to?

She told me about back pains and stomach cramps. She described an adoption agency that paid the medical bills and allowed her to screen parent profiles and name her baby. She held Stephanie in her arms once, and her mother snapped some pictures before the nurse came. She told me how Stephanie had turned her face to her breast and sucked the hospital gown. It made her think that humans should be marsupials, that we should have a pouch where we could grow in warmth and darkness, that nothing that fragile should have to face the world without the opportunity for retreat. When she's eighteen, she told me, they'll give her my name, she can look me up if she wants. Well, I said—I could think of nothing else to say—now I know why your mother flashes the porch light on and off.

We laughed too long at that—plainly, neither of us knew what to say. Then something made me mention the boys I'd had in college, and it was her turn to be beside me, silent. I told her that my problem seemed trivial compared to hers, but at least I understood it. I told her that I enjoyed anal intercourse, but when a boy pulled his penis out of me it felt like defecation. I really used these words; they seemed safely clinical. She told me that a woman she knew, on her fifth baby, said giving birth felt the same way: like taking a good shit. I felt she was offering me some kind of connection, but only a ladder's, and no matter how far I climbed, she would always be ahead of me.

After that we were beyond shyness, and we rolled close to

hold each other for warmth. I remember that I tried to make sense of everything that had just happened. I couldn't, but for some reason that didn't make me feel uncomfortable. I did understand one thing, though: she and I would never be lovers, and the strongest emotion that realization produced in me was relief. And I should tell you that that girl, of course, was Susan. But on the river that night, I didn't know what that would mean today, which is why I didn't reveal it before. Because knowing this, knowing the future, changes things, changes the past.

Susan's laughter coils like smoke through the air before reaching my ears. Bent over so that her shirt falls open, she rolls a second joint. "They make machines for that," I say. "Rolling joints?" she asks, laughing again. "Well, cigarettes, I suppose. But like most things, it does things it wasn't intended to." Her droll "Really" seems exaggerated; her follow-up— "Like assholes?"—surprises me. Trying to joke it off, I take the knife from the hummus. Susan's shoulder rubs mine as I bend next to her. "Like this," I say, and fake a stab. Her smile vanishes. She takes the knife and sets it on the table; the heavy clunk of metal on wood startles me. It's too easy, how the meanings of once-familiar actions change. Susan slips the joint in my mouth; "Such things are for people with clumsy fingers," she says as she lights it, and maybe it's because I've almost forgotten about the rolling machine, but when I've exhaled and she is still holding smoke in her lungs,

I say, "There's nothing wrong with my fingers," and run them along her arm. Susan's eyes lock on the space beyond my right shoulder. She exhales slowly. I've touched her a thousand times before; I do nothing to make this touch sexual. But the confusing blend of friendship and sexuality is inevitable. It is, after all, why we're here.

There was a time when I'd wanted to be powerless, and have sex. I wanted to lose control. I went to the Spike. I met Henry.

About forty then, defined by a decade of discos, gyms, and steroids, Henry wore leather pants and an unbuttoned button-down blue plaid shirt with the sleeves ripped off. A man's name, Lou, was tattooed on his shoulder, and his mustache was speckled gray. When he shook my hand my knuckles cracked. He bought me a beer, I bought him a beer, I told him what I wanted, he said, eventually, Do you have any limits? It was a Friday night; I said, I have to work Monday afternoon. And it's not enough to say he hurt me, to say that for two days and three nights he controlled me: I asked for that. He gave me something else, something I didn't understand until much later.

It was not, I think, in Henry's nature to hurt anyone. When I stroked his slick-leathered thigh in the taxi, he moaned; there was nothing dominant about it. If he'd had his way, we probably would have had sex normally, with perhaps a few accoutrements: a leather harness, latex gloves. But I insisted, and he knew what to do. We both did, we *all* did; we'd been taught, by people now mostly dead. So I submitted to his kissing, stripped for him, called him Master; on his order, I licked his boots. He collared me, attached a leash, led me on my knees to his bedroom. I was drawn but not quartered, tied to the four bedposts. My ass gripped his sheets and pulled them into my crack. The red-rubber-ball gag started out egg-sized, but soon became an orange in my mouth. He stuffed wax in my ears and I heard my breath come fast and shallow. He hooded me. And he knew, Henry. Before zipping the eye slits, he pulled a mirror from the wall and held it above me. I saw what I'd wanted to see: not myself, but a picture from a magazine. I was powerless, if not ridiculous. But I hadn't lost control. Then he closed the eye slits. They didn't seal completely, and I could see, if I shut one eye or the other, the jagged outline of the zipper and Henry's shadow as he moved about the room. Still, I was close enough to blind and nearly deaf from the wax. Bound, gagged, unable to do anything else, I waited.

S/M, if you let it, or if you can't stop it, delivers what it promises: pain that transforms. At first I understood things. I felt him handle my cock and balls; I could see, without looking, the thong stretching my balls away from my body and separating them from each other. It hurt, and my hips rocked a little in protest. The nipple clamps were two sharp pains that translated into two useless pulls against my bindings. When he twisted the clamps I tensed, trying not to resist, trying to be above the pain, but I realized that my head was rolling from side to side. And then I didn't know what was happening. Later I found he'd been pouring hot wax over my chest, stomach, balls, but then it just felt like my skin was on fire. I couldn't help myself, I struggled. The gag hadn't been a gag until the first time I tried to scream against it, and then it was. But even though I knew I couldn't speak, I continued to try, tried to force the gag from my mouth by the power of my breath alone.

It went on like this, until eventually I was just struggling. The pain ceased to have meaning in any real way. I simply wanted to be released, but I had no control over that. In realizing this, and accepting it, a wave of heat washed through me and seemed to separate my inner body from my skin. The pain, and the fighting, were outside me, and inside I was still. I barely noticed when Henry cut off my head and held it above my body so I could look again at myself. My skin, inflated like a balloon, was held to earth only by thin ties at the wrists and ankles. I smiled to think of my real self bouncing around freely inside, painless, weightless, like a child in the Moon Walk at the fair. My mind bounced too, from memory to memory, and all of them seemed somehow transformed into visions that, no matter how painful they might have been once, were now ecstatic, and it was wonderful, a kind of freedom from the past—it was what I wanted. And then he made me come. I felt his hand on my cock vaguely at first, not knowing what he was doing. But as he pumped I grew hard, the wax cooled, I forgot the tit clamps and cock-and-ball harness, and he kept pumping until eventually, inevitably, I came. And it was just like any other too-long-delayed orgasm: anticlimactic and tiring. I lay in my bonds, bored. And for two more days and two more nights I was bored, as Henry tried to think of ever more exciting things to torment and arouse me. Oh, it was amazing what he could do, and not draw blood.

And I remember asking him a totally inappropriate question once, when the gag was out of my mouth. Lou, I said, is he still alive? Henry scratched the tattoo as if he wished it would come off. Louise, he said, my ex-wife. Yes.

Susan bats at smoke, goes to open the windows. Worming my toes into the warm space where she'd sat, I close my eyes and lean back, only to jump forward when Susan sits on my feet. "My violet!" she says, pointing at my hands, immersed in a pot in her lap. "My feet!" I respond. She raises herself so I can move them, and I pull my fingers from her plant, a withered African violet. Brown-edged leaves hang from an aged, thick stem; dead ones line the pot. "I told him I'm no good with plants," she says, and when I realize she means Martin, I grab the pot again. "Maybe you should take it home." "Maybe I should." Sometimes I only understand people through objects, and in the solid unerotic shape of this plant I see Susan: were she truly trying to seduce me, she wouldn't have brought Martin into the room more than he already is. Already she's sliding across the couch. "I'd feel bad if it died." There's a hush after I say this; it's an old rule and now I've broken it: don't mention death around people who have lost someone. "Jesus, John," Susan says then, taking my hand, forcing me to look up from Martin's plant. "When you make love to me, please, don't think of him." Quiet after that, broken only by the sound of the plant being set on the table. What's truly remarkable, I suppose, isn't that it's dying, but that it lived this long. We stare at each other in silence. And it's like the first time: when the silence becomes uncomfortable, we kiss, and then, for just a moment, I hear water running somewhere close by.

Sometimes sex is perfect. I remember my fourth time with Martin, the first time we fucked. I remember the fourth time because that's when I fell for him. Something held us back our first three times; our minds were elsewhere, our hands could have been tied. But the fourth time. There we were: Martin's place, Martin's old couch. There we were: Martin and John. The two of us, 3 a.m., empty bottles on the coffee table. We had exhausted conversation, wine had exhausted us, we stared at the TV. It was turned off. How did he do it? I mean, I know what he did: he put his hand on my leg. He didn't look at me when he did it, just lifted his right hand off his right leg and set it down on my left one, just above my knee. Just above my knee, and then it slid up my thigh, slowly, but not wasting time. That's what he did. But how did he make my diaphragm contract so tightly that I couldn't take one breath for the entire minute it took his hand to move to my belt? My stomach was so tight a penny would have bounced off it. His fingers found the belt buckle, worked it, a small sound of metal on metal, a sudden release, a rush of air—my lungs' air—and my pants were open and I gasped for breath.

Martin put his hand back in his lap. His words, when they came, were even. He could have been talking about the weather. You could slip a condom on your cock, he said, and twirl me on it like a globe on its axis. The words took shape in the room; they made sex seem as understandable as pornography. On the blank TV screen I imagined I saw Martin and myself, fucking. I looked down at my open pants, at my underwear, white as a sheet of paper. Or I could do you, he said. Still, I hesitated, not because I didn't want him, but because the very thought of fucking Martin added so many possibilities to my life that I grew dizzy contemplating them. Just do what you want to do, Martin said, but do it now. I kissed him. I pulled open the buttons of his shirt, pushed down his pants. I bent over him and ran my tongue over his chest, into his navel, down to his cock and balls. When I got there I swabbed the shaft until it glistened. I rolled his balls around my mouth the way a child rolls marbles in his hand. And it's important to know that I didn't do this because I suddenly loved him. I just wanted to fuck. Do it, I whispered. Do it.

And he did, lying on the floor, on a rug, though I didn't twirl as easily as those globes in high school, and in fact, after one revolution, I didn't twirl at all, but sat astride him and rocked up and down. And he pumped, pumped like anyone in any skinflick ever made, though I didn't think of that then, but only of the amazing sensation of having this man inside me. A funny thing happened then. He pumped and I rocked, and I rocked and he pumped, and eventually our rhythm must have been just right, for the rug, a small Persian carpet–type thing patterned in tangled growing vines, came out from under us as if it had been pulled. I fell over, he slipped out of me, we ended up on our sides, side by side, laughing. We lay on the floor for a long time, mouths open, our stomachs heaving as we sucked in air. We touched each other only with our fingertips, and then only slightly, and we lay on the floor for a long time, laughing.

We finished on his bed. I don't remember going there, just a point at which the world returned like a shadow and I saw my cum splashed on his stomach and legs, and his splashed on mine, and below us was a white sheet instead of the rug. Then for a moment I wanted to take everything a step further. I wanted to run my finger through Martin's cum and lick the finger clean. But Martin smiled at me. He kissed me. When my hands went for his body, he caught them halfway and held them. In a light voice he said, In my experience, there are two kinds of men in the world: those who play with their lover's hair when they're getting a blowjob, and those who play with their own. Though I tried, I couldn't remember what I'd done. Which type am I? I asked. You, he said, and showed me as he told me, put one hand on my head, and one on yours. And which are you? Martin looked at my hair. If there was a mirror handy, he said, you wouldn't have to ask that question. His words didn't really *mean* anything, but they accomplished what I think he meant them to: I forgot my desire to taste his cum. He lifted the sheet then and fluffed it with his arms, like wings, then let it settle on our shoulders, and I didn't realize we were standing up until I awoke hours later.

After that he could have asked me to do anything. A caress from Martin had more strength than any punch Henry would ever land. But he rarely used this power, and I suppose I had the same control over him. Didn't he, as well, sleep standing in my arms? We shut the windows, turned off the phone, unplugged the clock. We wore no clothes for days, and used our time to make love, to eat and sleep. What I remember from that time, the time we shut out the world, is sweating on his bed as he dove into me, and someone somewhere flushing a toilet and the wall behind Martin's bed rattling as water rushed through pipes concealed within it.

Just after that time I asked Susan what pregnancy was like. She'd been talking, vaguely, about having a baby, though she said she couldn't name five straight men in the world that she'd want to father it. If you've ever had a cock moving deep inside you, you know that it can feel like a part of you, even as you realize that it belongs to him. Can you imagine this staying in you after he pulls out, staying, growing, moving around eventually, making its presence, its separate life, known? This is how I imagined pregnancy. I asked Susan if this was reasonable. She sighed and smiled. Not even close, she said. Not even close.

When her shirt comes off, I'm struck by the strength in Susan's shoulders. Instead of unbuttoning it, she pulls it over her head, and her hair falls back audibly to surround her thin neck. Sometimes I think it's Susan, and not Martin, who is the love of my life. I don't know why I believe in such a concept—perhaps because thinking it distracts me from the larger fact: that I can have neither of them. Except for Susan, except for tonight. And that other night: I remember the river, both of us tenderly helping the other off with clothes. Tonight we kiss for a while, then stop, come to the bedroom. In here, candles instead of electric light or darkness, windows open but curtains drawn, so that they move in the breeze. Incense. The music from the other room. Susan busies herself with setting the stage, and then we pull our clothes off alone and pretend to ignore each other. But Susan, folding her bra in half, catches my eye. "There's an extra toothbrush if you want to brush your teeth," she says, and looks away. I have to fight back laughter. I know the kind of laughter it would be, cynical laughter, sad laughter, having more to do with things outside this room than in it. I feel like something's been stolen from me. I want to compliment her, tell her I think she's beautiful. At the river, I could have done so—I did, because the sex we had then was, we thought, just between the two of us. And it's not that Susan is no longer beautiful, no longer sexual. But her sexuality exists apart from me. Her apartment, these trappings, are one thing; she'll play with them. But not with herself. Not tonight. Tonight I'm not her lover. I'm just helping her to have her baby.

When she first came to us, only Martin and I knew he was sick. We'd known for months, but were still unwilling to give his illness the legitimacy, the finality, of a name. She presented her plan: she would have a baby and raise it alone. Perhaps one day she would marry, but she didn't foresee it and she didn't particularly care. She was happy fucking around: she wanted a baby, not a husband. But she didn't want anonymous sperm or the hassle of a turkey baster, and she couldn't afford artificial insemination. She wanted to do it the old-fashioned way. And she wanted to make love to me. I asked what she expected of me, besides sperm. Uncle John, she said. You will be Uncle John, and this one here will be Uncle Martin. She must have wondered why she laughed alone at her joke.

Before she left she asked him if he'd lost weight. After she left he said he was cold. In the bedroom I curled up with him under the blanket. Then he was hot and wanted to throw the blanket off, but I suggested we take our clothes off instead.

And then he was cold again, and I took him in my arms and rolled us in the blanket, and when I'd finished we were pressed together front to front and I opened my mouth and closed it over his and tickled his lips with my tongue until he let me in. And then he pulled back and said, You shouldn't, and I looked into his face, so pale that it seemed almost greenish, and I said, I should, and kissed him again.

Wrapped in the blanket, stretched out on the bed, we could have been suspended in space. By our feet, by our heads, by our cocks, suspended in time. I reached down and pushed my cock between his sweating thin legs and pulled his between mine. Sometimes when we did it that way I imagined that I was inside him, but that night I imagined I was inside a woman. That was the only way he'd let us do it anymore, he said my health has got to be protected, said he loves me too much to kill me, said anything to keep me away from him because now, now that he's sick, he's afraid of what he wants because he's afraid of what he wanted because he thinks that what he wanted not what he did is why he's going to die.

When at last we unrolled the blanket, it seemed that buckets of salty-sweet water rolled off the bed as the last fold parted. Though untouched, the sheets were soaked, and I remade the bed before joining Martin in the shower. His thin back was bent over a fern he kept on the deep window ledge; his fingers pulled a few brown leaves from the pot and let them fall in the tub. Because you love me, he said. And because you love her. I said, What? He said, I think you should, if you can, if you stay healthy, you should help Susan. After I'm dead.

After he said that, I didn't do laundry for two weeks, didn't do anything, and when I came across those sheets again they were wet as if we'd used them just minutes ago, and covered in places with a thin green layer of mold. I held them in my hand and felt their green sliminess stick to my fingers and I didn't know what to think: if this was the product of fucking Martin, or if this was the product of nothing, or, worst of all, if this, the product of fucking Martin, was nothing.

After he died I didn't tell anyone for fifteen hours. I left his body in the hospital bed in the living room through the day, pulled back the covers once and looked at it, and then pulled them up to cover what was there. From seven in the morning until ten at night. I might have left him like that forever, but Susan came over to check on us. I brought her into the apartment and sat her down, and then I walked over to Martin and kissed him on the lips. They didn't taste like him. Nothing happened. I looked at Susan. She was crying; I remembered that she'd known him longer than I had, that she'd introduced us. I said, I wanted to do that in front of someone, so that when he didn't wake up, I'd know he was dead. And after Martin's body was gone and his bed sat there empty because they pick up bodies any time but they only pick up beds between nine and five, weekdays, I sent Susan away and then I went out myself. The air was hot and dry, the only moisture spat by air conditioners. I didn't want to be alone with my grief, I wanted to give it to someone, to the whole city. I stopped a man on the street, put my hand right on his chest. Martin, I started, but the man ran away. Didn't he know I could never hurt him? I walked a long time, until I had no place else to go, and so I went to the Spike, where I met Henry.

Two years have passed.

In this world, Susan says, there's as much nihilism in having a baby as in having one by me. I can't argue with that.

Science says I have nothing to protect her from. But still.

Part of the arrangement with the adoption agency was that every year, on Stephanie's birthday, Susan received an update on her daughter's life. The letters, addressed "Dear Birth Mother" and signed "The Adopted Parents," were always short, and came with two or three severely cropped polaroids of Stephanie. Only fragments of bodies—hands, the side of a leg—indicated that she didn't live alone. When Susan moved from Kansas she didn't leave a forwarding address with the agency.

The situation presses against me like . . . like what? Like trampling feet? Like uplifting hands? We weren't prepared for this—any of this. There are times when the past overwhelms the present, and nothing will happen, and there are also times when the present overwhelms the past, and nothing that happens makes sense. Here, today, the equations are changed: silence equals death, they teach us, and action equals life. And though I no longer question these anymore, I sometimes wonder, Whose death? Whose life?

Martin's life resided in his right hand. He pointed it out to me with his left; his right hand rested on my thigh and he said: Look. I looked for a long time and then, just when I was about to ask what I was looking for, I saw it, his pulse, visibly beating in the blue trace of a vein in the patch of skin where his thumb and forefinger met. For a moment I considered pressing my own finger on it, as a joke. I don't remember if this was before or after we knew he had AIDS. I don't remember if I put my finger on the vein.

Mouth open, teeth resting against Susan's inner thigh just above her knee, I stop what I'm doing as I realize I'm crying. My body trembles slightly. I feel, don't see, Susan's head lift up. "Dale?" she whispers.

Then John puts his hand on her pussy, where soon he will insert his dick and for all intents and purposes plant his seed; he runs fingers through her bush and teases her clit, and her head sinks to the pillow. She can't see his face or the tears streaming down it. He remembers suddenly what he wanted to tell that man on the street: Martin, he would have said, Martin is dead. Martin is *so* dead. And he remembers a piece of sado-babble that Henry had whispered to him. You will never be free of me, Henry had said, and John realizes that, though this isn't true of Henry, it is true of Martin. And Susan. Even more than he fears what he's doing now, he fears what will happen when Susan finds someone else, falls in love, leaves him. He admits something to himself that he's always known but never accepted: that he wasn't her first lover—just as she wasn't his—and that they won't be each other's last, as well. That, even as his passion for Martin has become this lament, his grief, too, will pass away, and Martin will be even more dead. And whatever else happens, the person that may or may not have been conceived tonight won't be Martin.

The sum of life isn't experience, I realize, isn't something that can be captured with words. Inevitably, things have been left out. Perhaps they appear in others' stories. Perhaps they were here once and John's forgotten them. Perhaps some things he remembers didn't really occur. But none of that matters now. Even as Susan takes John inside her he knows that this baby means something, though I've fought against that; even Martin has become something abstract. A symbol, like the rose John once put in Martin's lapel, like Susan's African violet, like the fern in the shower. But after tonight, Martin's face will be inseparable from Susan's, from John's own, which is just a mask for mine. How can this story give Martin immortality when it can't even give him life? Now I wonder, Has this story liberated anything but my tears? And is that enough? I want to ask. To which I can only answer, Isn't that enough?

I thought I'd controlled everything so well, the plants, Martin, John, Susan. Even the semen.

In this story, I'd intended semen to be the water of life.

But, in order to live, I've only ever tasted mine.

I DIVIDE MY LIFE

IN TWO

▌

*I divide my life in two: before Martin, and after Martin. There
are many places I could make the division: before my mother's
death and after, before I ran away from home and after. Before,
and after. But Martin. I loved him. That's nothing—if someone is weak enough, or strong enough, I'll love them. But he
loved me back. Now, I feel the lack of him every day. Oh, he
hated me at the end. Every day he wished aloud that I would
get sick and die before he did. But I never stopped loving him.
I won't say he didn't hurt me. There were times when I got
picked up and stayed away for two or three days, so that when
I came home Martin would clutch me and beg for forgiveness.
The sight of him always filled me with guilt. Within minutes
Martin picked up on this and turned cold on me. Now, if I
think about him for too long, I get tired. I go to the bedroom
then, and I use only one pillow and I ball up the blanket and
I hold it in my arms, and I tell myself the only thing I know:
that my life is divided in two now, irrevocably, by a chasm*

as wide and deep and unfillable as any canyon. But I still can't decide if that chasm is Martin's life, or if it's his death.

I live by a routine now. Every morning I wake, usually without the alarm, which is set for nine, and I get up and I feed the cat and I take my vitamins, which sit on the shelf next to a bottle of AZT which I haven't needed yet, and then I make and drink a pot of tea. While I'm drinking it I decide what I'm going to do during the day, besides write, and when I've decided, and when I've finished my tea, I take a brief shower, just enough to wash the sleep from my eyes and the dust from my skin, and then I go back to the kitchen to wash the morning dishes, mine, and the cat's as well, if it's finished eating. The cat strayed in. It came by during the winter, thin and shivering, and I fed it so much that now it's become fat and lazy, and so I've put it on a diet and feed it only twice a day. Already it's begun to lose weight. As I watch it become slimmer, more active, I think that if people had such a controlling force in their lives then there wouldn't be half as much chaos as there is. Sometimes I think that the cat is my controlling force. I could sleep late these days, but I don't: instead, I awaken to the sound of the cat calling for its food and the smell of dust. It's summer, and by ten the last of the dew has burned off, and it's a year since Martin died.

Sometimes you have to start over. The stories you make up for yourself don't seem to have any relevance to the life you lead; the horrors you imagined pale beside the ones you experience, and in your mind there's a battle as it tries to find something to grab on to, whether it's a memory of something that happened or a memory of something you imagined, a story you told yourself. I remember making up my first stories at night, kept awake by the sound of my parents fighting in the other room. Every fiction is always opposed to some truth, and the opposition in these stories was easy to spot, for they were about a happy mother, happy father, happy John. But this changed. Soon the stories I imagined were as horrible as the one I lived. I found a power in it, and that power increased as the imagined horror became more and more like the events of my life. You can search for a meaning in that. I tell myself that by reinventing my life, my imagination imposes an order on things and makes them make sense. But sometimes I think that horror is all I know and all I'll ever know, and no matter how much I try to loose my mind from the bonds and the boundaries of the events of my life, it returns to them always, obsessively, like a dog sniffing for a bone it buried too deep and now can't find.

I write during the afternoon. Martin told me to. I don't think that's why I do it now, but he started me. Now I write because I can't stop, but now isn't so far from the days when I couldn't start, when the thought of trying to get it out, to get it all down, seemed like such an enormous undertaking that I couldn't even pick up a pen. Martin fell ill less than six months after we got together, but in my memory it feels *like this happened a long time before. I remember that we lay in bed, we'd just made love or we were about to, and I was trying to figure out how I'd gotten there. Not just to Martin's bed, but to that place in my life. I'm still trying to figure that out, how I got here, and only recently have I begun to wonder where I am. I remember I started thinking aloud, and before I knew it I was telling Martin all these things I thought I'd forgotten. I told him about my hand, and about a man named Harry, and about a warm November day at the beach, and none of it made sense. None of it followed. And Martin asked me then if I'd ever thought of writing it down, a piece at a time if I had to, and putting those pieces in order, and of course I answered no.*

Memory is my only possession, but it resists ownership. I remember the first thing I wrote: this is the worst thing I remember, I wrote, and then I stopped writing. Nothing came after that sentence; nothing ever did. Nothing announced itself as the worst of it all, although many, many things—images, sounds, sensations, sentences even, though I don't remember who first wrote or spoke them—all vied for the honor. So I abandoned that first effort and I started again. I wrote: this is not the worst thing I remember, and then, I don't know why, but I wrote something that hadn't happened. Every-thing's been a little confused since then, what's real and what's invented, but it all seems to make more sense too.

In the evenings I run errands. I'm always surprised when I remember how long I've lived here. Three years. People rec-

ognize me, they know my name. "Hi, John," says Tillie, the sixty-year-old woman who rings up my groceries for me. "Hi, Tillie," I say, and then we each say a few things, usually about the weather, to fill up the minute or so it takes her to check me out. In the evening, after I've finished writing, I often just sit on the porch and watch the sun set over the field across from my house. I watch the sun set a lot. I look for flaws, for something to mar that beauty. How can someone trust those colors? I sometimes wonder why the air doesn't collapse under their weight. In the red light I can just make out the grass waving in the wind, and I watch it bend in the air, and then sway back, and then bend forward again, end-lessly, and I watch until it grows too dark for me to see, and then I go inside. Inside, there is the cat to be fed, and me, and while I eat I usually read over what I've written. I see it differently the second time around. It's like I've taken a puzzle, a jigsaw puzzle, and put it together all wrong, so that none of the pieces fit into each other, but are forced together or merely laid end to end. I look down on the picture that is supposed to be rectangular, but is circular. It glows with color. I see within it the barn it was supposed to be, but I see more too. The barn shifts, shimmers, changes before me in a way I can't follow: it becomes a house for people, not animals, and then a mausoleum for the dead, not the living. Still, it has a definite shape. Though I can't put my finger on any particular piece and give it a name, I can look at it and know what it is. It's enough that way, the knowing without touching, without understanding, without dissecting. And then, when I've finished eating and I've finished reading, I wind the clock and I go to bed. It's one of those new clocks made to seem old-fashioned: it's round, with two bells mounted on top and a hammer poised between, and I keep it only because the other clock in the house is digital and when the power goes out I have no way to tell what time it is.

Already I know it's not enough. Already I feel myself becoming bored. I've been idle for a year now and it's all begun to grow off me, the smell of dust, the sight of long grass rolling in a breeze. I'm used to things happening. But I'm afraid too. If I have nothing else right now, I have control, and I don't want to risk losing that by doing something, meeting a man, making a friend, getting a job. I know I'll have to do something eventually, but right now there's just the bedroom, and that's enough for me, the bedroom and the bed and the idea of sleep. One morning I'll wake up and I won't do something I always do, and then I'll know it's time to make the change; or else I just won't wake up and that will be that. Sometimes in those last minutes before sleep my heart feels like a blood-filled bellows, and if I turn and look at Martin's side of the bed, I can see it beside me. It labors mightily, inflating and deflating, and each time it deflates it spews out a viscous pool of blood which spills everywhere, and all I have ever felt is love and hate, rage and joy, terror and numbness, and there is no center to any of these spectra, only north and south poles which I sway between like a pendulum which exists only at *its two high points. Nothing I know tells me that life can be any different from this, nothing except for the experience of these last few months, when there have been no high points, no polar opposites, no extremes of emotion, and it's as if I've ceased to exist. Everything tells me that if I want to survive I have to find a middle ground, a place where I can stand and not feel as if on one side a sea rages to consume me and on the other side a vast open prairie waits deceptively to engulf me in immense emptiness. I don't know what the place is I'm looking for, I only know what it's not, and it's not that, it's not all or nothing. It's something, but it's not that.*